BEAUTIFULLY TORN

CANDIED CRUSH #16

CHARITY PARKERSON

—Warning: This book is intended for readers over the age of 18.

Copyright © 2021 Charity Parkerson
Editor: BZ Hercules & Consultants
ISBN: 978-1-946099-88-4
All rights reserved.

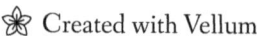 Created with Vellum

INTRODUCTION

MOST PEOPLE SPEND YEARS LOOKING FOR THEIR SOUL MATE. JINX HAS MORE CHOICES THAN HE CAN HANDLE.

Working for Zealous Blaze has opened a world of sexy men for Jinx. On one hand, he has a rock star. On the other, the head of security for a billionaire. Jinx has never been more torn in his life.

Hudson can have any man he wants. Fame turns a lot of heads. The only guy he wants for more than one night doesn't want him back. It's a position he's never been in before. It's definitely not a place he thought he would fight to stay in. Yet here he is.

Rocky has better things to do than fight for the attention of guy who's way too young for him. He can't stop. Jinx is everything Rocky has searched for his entire life. He's also Rocky's best friend. It's a mess he doesn't know how to escape.

Two men fighting for the same heart is a situation bound to end in heartache for someone. Or maybe not.

ONE

WHEN HUDSON VINCENT walked through a crowd, heads turned. Phones appeared in people's hands and lights popped from where people forgot to turn off the flash on their cameras. Hudson ran his fingers through his bright green hair that was shaved down the sides, flipping his mohawk to one side. Jinx smiled as he watched Hudson pretend not to notice the way everyone took his picture while he made his way through the restaurant. Light glimmered off the ring in his nose and lip. His heavily lined lids made the boredom in his green eyes even more obvious. Jinx wondered how much of his expression was an act. The only thing keeping anyone from throwing their underwear Hudson's way was the bodyguard shielding his every step. Hudson moved like he didn't even notice he was being shadowed.

"Do you plan to walk right by me like you don't even see me?"

Hudson glanced Jinx's way like he planned to keep moving, blowing off whoever dared to say such a thing to him. When his gaze landed on Jinx, his expression changed. Happiness flashed in his eyes. Butterflies stirred in Jinx's gut. Hudson had a way of making Jinx feel special, but Jinx refused to show it. After all, Hudson was a grunge rock god. Jinx was no one. Yet, somehow, they were still friends.

"Jinx. Wow. I really didn't see you there, but now that I have, how could I walk right by your gorgeous self?"

Jinx rolled his eyes before he could stop himself.

. . .

A bright smile lit Hudson's features at Jinx's reaction. "You're the only person I know who rolls their eyes at every compliment. Do you think you're surrounded by liars?"

"I know I am."

Hudson threw his head back and roared with laughter. He plopped down in the seat across from Jinx without an invitation. "You're so much fun. Are you eating alone?"

"I am."

Hudson's eyes flashed with mischief. "Mhmm. I do love having you to myself."

Jinx's heart skipped a beat. He had felt that hum against his skin before. It was pretty fucking amazing. As sound engineer for Zealous Blaze, the top DJ in the world, Jinx had met a ton of celebrities.

Most were horrible and ignored Jinx. He was beneath them. Jinx had been beneath Hudson in a whole other way more than once. It was a magical place to be. Jinx knew better than to let someone like Hudson see him starstruck.

Hudson set his elbow on the table and propped up his chin with his fist. His gaze never wavered from Jinx. "Where's that big-ass guard of yours?"

"If you mean Rocky, he's not my guard, and he's working." Hudson had met Rocky at the last rave Jinx worked. Now Hudson brought him up every time they saw each other.

The laughter flashing in Hudson's eyes said he heard the forced disinterest in Jinx's voice and planned to exploit it. "I'm well aware he works for your boss's man, but you live with them, right?"

It was true Jinx lived with Zayn and Spencer... and Rocky, but Jinx didn't see Hudson's point. "Yes, but that still doesn't make Rocky my guard. He's head of Zayn's security team."

"You two are together a lot."

Jinx leaned closer as he spotted his chance to turn the tables. "Are you jealous?"

Hudson dropped his arm and leaned closer too. "Should I be? Does he know how you sound when you come?"

An unexpected wave of longing washed over Jinx. No one knew how much he wanted the sexy guard he spent his nights talking and laughing with. Still, he couldn't let Hudson see his weakness. "Nope. You hold that distinction."

"Damn. He has no idea what he's missing."

. . .

"Would you like me to move your meal to this table, Mr. Vincent?"

The server's sudden appearance and question had Jinx sitting back in his seat. He hadn't realized Hudson had been sitting elsewhere in the restaurant.

Hudson nodded. "That sounds great. Thanks."

The server moved away, and Jinx watched as she picked up a plate and drink from a crowded table. The three men at the table watched as the server brought the plate to Jinx's table. Then their heads came together, obviously discussing their abandonment. "Won't your friends miss you?" Jinx asked as his gaze moved back Hudson's way. He found Hudson staring.

Hudson shrugged. "I'd rather be with you."

. . .

Jinx hated the way his chest warmed at the claim. He wasn't dumb enough to think he could hold Hudson's attention for long. Jinx hated that he wanted it nonetheless. His life was a bit fucked up. Jinx wanted the man seated across from him. Not the rock star, but the man. Yet he also craved the sexy guard at home. He never dreamed it would feel every bit as unlucky to desire two men as it felt to be completely unwanted. Jinx wasn't sure this problem wasn't worse. On one hand, he could let Hudson completely level his life. On the other, Rocky likely didn't want him at all. Jinx didn't know which limb to climb out on. Each one seemed just as likely to break. It was a conundrum. Hudson swept a heated gaze over Jinx, and Jinx settled in. If he was doomed to get hurt no matter what he chose, there was no sense in thinking too hard. He may as well go down moaning.

The amount of stress Rocky felt when Jinx went anywhere alone was well beyond what could be considered healthy. Rocky couldn't help it. He was protective by nature, and it was Jinx. Jinx was young and sweet. He was off limits to everyone as far as

Rocky was concerned, especially to Rocky. Jinx was like family to Rocky's boss, Zayn. Since Zayn would soon be married to Jinx's boss, Spencer, that made Spencer Rocky's boss too. They were one big chosen family. Rocky would die for every last one of them. Plus, Rocky had been a thug in a former life, he was ten years older than Jinx, and there was just no way they would ever be together.

As if thinking about him conjured him, Jinx came through the door. Rocky swore a fire lit in his chest at the first sight of his shaggy-haired boy. His light blue gaze landed on Rocky and a smile lit his face. At the first glimpse of his adorable smile, Rocky almost ran toward him, greeting him like a fucking dog. Then Hudson came through the door on Jinx's heels. Rocky's smile dimmed.

"You brought home company."

Jinx nodded. "I ran into Hudson at lunch. We got to talking and had a great idea for a project. Since we're both free today, we're running with it."

. . .

Rocky didn't hear half of what Jinx said. The way Hudson looked at Jinx distracted the hell out of Rocky. Before Rocky could formulate a halfway intelligent response, Jinx started down the hall toward his bedroom.

Rocky followed. "If you're only working, wouldn't that be easier in the living room?"

A low chuckle floated down the hall. "I'm not twelve, Rocky. I'm allowed to have boys in my room."

Hudson followed Jinx to the door of his bedroom. At the last second, he turned and eyed Rocky from head to toe while walking backward into Jinx's bedroom. "You should join us."

"If you're only working, why should I join you?" Rocky didn't blink as he posed the question.

. . .

Hudson didn't back down either. He smirked. "Would you join us if we weren't?"

A wave of possessiveness overwhelmed Rocky. He wanted to mark his territory. "Leave the door open."

Hudson's smile kicked up a notch. "Why? Do you want to watch?"

"For fuck's sake." Jinx moved between them and closed the door in Rocky's face. Rocky pressed his forehead against the wood, fighting the urge to kick it down.

"What are you doing?"

At Zayn's sudden appearance, Rocky jumped away from the door. "Nothing. I was just..."

· · ·

Zayn made a dismissive gesture. "Never mind. I've been looking for you. Spencer and I need to go over a few things with you."

Since Zayn hadn't called him on his weirdo behavior, Rocky dutifully followed Zayn down the hall. He forced himself not to look back. Hudson probably already had Jinx halfway undressed by now. Rocky focused on Zayn to keep from going insane. Zayn wasn't particularly tall. Of course, everyone was shorter than Rocky. Except for Spencer, who Rocky could already see was waiting for them outside the dining room. As they headed inside the dining room, Zayn motioned for him to sit. Rocky's anxiety shot through the roof. He had been acting like a crazed stalker lately and likely fucking up on the job. It hadn't occurred to him until now that Zayn might not put up with this shit for long. He wondered if they were firing him or planned to make him move out. After all, Jinx was important to them. Rocky was just some guy who had gotten busted stealing a car from Zayn. He definitely wasn't worth keeping. Zayn was crazy for having kept him this long.

. . .

Zayn pulled a planner closer and tapped it with a pen. "We've been looking over the schedule, trying to free up more time for you. With the wedding coming up, we'll be crazy busy with tuxedo measurements and parties. Obviously, we want you there as a guest. Not working. Who on your team do you want to promote?"

"Um..." Rocky hadn't been prepared. He'd had a completely different notion of where this meeting was going, especially since he was the one who usually set his team's schedule.

"I'm still planning to pay you your regular salary. This isn't cutting into your check."

At the misunderstanding, Rocky forced his mind on track. "Corey is my best guy. Plus, he has a baby on the way. If anyone deserves the promotion and needs the extra money, it's him."

. . .

Spencer nodded, as if he approved, while Zayn jotted in his notebook. Zayn didn't look up as he spoke. "Obviously, it's your team, so you can let him know and set his new wages. I'll give you a list of dates that I need him covering for you. We have a designer coming next Wednesday to get started on our tuxes. You'll need to be available."

Rocky glanced over his shoulder. He hoped this didn't take long. It was supposed to be his day off, and he didn't want to miss seeing Jinx again. "Yeah. I'll be here."

"You two should just fuck."

Rocky's head whipped back around at Spencer's words. "I'm sorry, what?"

Spencer looked like a Viking with his blond hair, beard, and blue eyes. Sometimes, his stare looked like it cut right through Rocky. Today was one of those days. Adding to Rocky's surprise, Zayn was the one who repeated Spencer's claim. "He's talking about Jinx. You two should just fuck and get it over with. The tension in this house is making everyone crazy."

For a moment, Rocky eyed Zayn, wondering if he had lost his mind. The same light brown eyes that had saved him fifteen years ago stared him every bit as steadily now. Zayn was of Asian descent, was smart as hell, and highly pragmatic. He was also one hundred percent serious. Rocky didn't know what to say. He chose the most obvious path.

"I work here, and Jinx is like family."

"To us," Spencer said, confusing Rocky. "He's like family to us," Spencer clarified, obviously seeing the bewilderment on Rocky's face. "You're perfectly free to fuck him. Both of you are adults. Just get it over with. No one cares."

He did. Before he could say as much, the sound of Hudson and Jinx coming down the hall distracted him. He glanced over his shoulder, desperately trying to catch a glimpse. Surely they hadn't finished already. If that was all the time Hudson dedicated to Jinx, then maybe Rocky should be the one fucking him.

Zayn let out a loud sigh. "Just go."

Rocky turned back the couple's way, determined to pay attention. "It's fine. Finish your spiel."

With a shake of his head, Zayn closed his notebook. "Go before you miss him. Just don't forget about Wednesday."

Rocky flew to his feet. "Yep. Wednesday. Got it." He was down the hall before he finished making his promise. Jinx wore different clothes. Otherwise, he looked unmolested.

. . .

"Hey. Are you leaving again?" It was a dumb question. They were obviously headed out.

Hudson held up the camera he carried. "Jinx came up with a great plan for an urban photo shoot for a hardback glossy accompaniment book to go with my next album—like a collector's thing. We're headed to Spencer's place in the warehouse district to get started. You should come with."

Rocky geared up to immediately say no, but Jinx's face lit. "That's a great idea. You'd make an amazing model."

Hudson nodded. "You really would. Plus, if I put you two together, yum. People will be licking the pages. Come on." Hudson headed for the door, as if it was settled.

Still, Rocky dragged his feet. He didn't think spending the day with Hudson and Jinx together was such a good idea. Then Jinx took his hand. Rocky's legs carried him in Jinx's direction. He would go wherever Jinx wanted him to go, as long as Jinx didn't let go. Outside, a large, black SUV with dark tinted windows sat waiting. As soon as Rocky closed the front door behind them, the driver's side and passenger side doors opened. Two gigantic men in black suits stepped out, opening the back doors. Hudson circled the vehicle. He climbed into one side while Jinx dragged Rocky into the other. The leather bench seat was surprisingly roomy and comfortable. Still, they seemed squished together once the doors closed, shutting them inside. Rocky recognized it was his large frame taking up all the space. He draped his arm across the back of the seat, freeing up some room. To his surprise, Jinx leaned his way. He set his hand on Rocky's knee.

Hudson held the floor, chatting the entire way to the warehouse district. Rocky didn't hear a word. His entire being stayed focused on Jinx's hand. It was such a small thing. Rocky's skin burned with desire. He had never been more spatially aware. It felt like it took forever to get to Spencer's warehouse. Rocky had to keep stopping himself from leaning closer to smell Jinx's cologne. He nearly leaped from the car when it stopped. Hudson's bodyguard looked more than a little surprised when Rocky not only didn't wait for him to open the door, but also almost took him out with it. Rocky flashed the huge bald dude a smile.

"Sorry. I'm not used to anyone opening my door."

Jinx climbed out behind him, and Rocky automatically turned to help. He didn't realize what he had done until Jinx accepted his hand and then didn't let go. Rocky's entire being stayed focused the rest of the day on every way Jinx touched him. Then he read too much into each encounter. Hudson took several photos of the walls tagged with spray paint. He positioned Jinx in different poses before turning his attention Rocky's way.

Rocky fought a blush. "No. Thanks, but you don't want me in this thing."

. . .

"Don't be hardheaded," Hudson said, rolling his eyes.

Jinx snagged the belt loops of Rocky's jeans and walked backward, dragging Rocky into the frame. His mischievous smile was all Rocky could see. "Come on. Don't be shy. Hudson plans to pay you really, really well for this. Plus, don't you want to play with me?" Rocky didn't know what that meant, but he still held still while Jinx unbuttoned his shirt. Jinx kept his gaze locked on his task. "You're the only man I know who wears twill button-down shirts on their day off." He ran his fingertip down Rocky's forearm. "I love the way you roll the sleeves to your elbows, though."

Too late, Rocky realized his shirt was open and Hudson had been snapping pictures all along.

When the sun began to set, Hudson dragged them outside. He positioned Jinx and Rocky with the setting sun to one side while he took pictures from the other, letting the sunset be their background.

Hudson had them facing each other. Every few seconds, he moved them closer. Rocky stared into Jinx's sexy light blue eyes and forgot why they were there.

"Now lean in like you're about to kiss."

Rocky tried looking Hudson's way to argue. Jinx touched Rocky's face and drew him closer. He stopped an inch away from Rocky's mouth. Rocky's lips parted on a breath. His eyes automatically fell closed while his heartbeat pounded in his ears. He wanted to close the final gap as much as he craved his next breath.

"Perfect. You two look like you belong together. This needs a little something extra, though. Tito, come take this camera."

At Hudson's words, Rocky came back to reality and took a step back. His heart rate didn't slow, and his lust didn't ebb. Jinx looked dazed and turned on. Rocky couldn't look away.

Hudson passed the camera to the huge guard Rocky had almost nailed with the door. Then he joined them in the pictures. Jinx and Hudson exchanged a glance and a smile. Before he grasped their intentions, they sandwiched Rocky between them. Jinx moved behind Rocky, grabbed both halves of his shirt, and tugged. Rocky automatically leaned back into Jinx's arms as Jinx exposed his chest and trapped his upper arms in the material. The clicking of the camera was the only sound filling the air as Jinx's mouth opened against the side of Rocky's neck. Rocky's head fell back. A gasp escaped him. Hudson's body melded against him. His lips touched Rocky's collarbone. Rocky saw stars. He became hyper aware of every place they touched. They were all hard. He knew there was no way Hudson missed his erection since he was fully aware of theirs. Rocky had two tongues stroking his skin, and it was too much. He wanted to fuck. There was a bed inside the warehouse. Rocky wanted to be there right now, between these bodies. He didn't doubt for a moment they would be explosive. Then it was over.

. . .

Hudson moved away and reclaimed the camera. As he flipped through the images, Jinx fixed Rocky's shirt. Rocky stared at Jinx, willing him to say something as he buttoned Rocky's shirt for him. When the tension became too much, Rocky's mouth opened. Confessions raced to his tongue.

"These pictures are amazing, guys," Hudson said, saving Rocky from himself. "You both did fantastic."

Jinx took Rocky's hand and headed for the SUV. "Please send me copies of the best shots. This was so much fun."

Tito opened the door. Rocky did his best not to make eye contact as he followed Jinx into the backseat. This time, once they were closed inside, an odd sense of intimacy washed over Rocky. They felt shut away from the rest of the world. It was like they were in their own bubble. Rocky draped his arm over Jinx's shoulders instead of the seat. Jinx set his hand on Rocky's thigh. Hudson turned Jinx's way and draped his arm across the back of the seat. His hand came to rest on Rocky's shoulder. He stroked. Back and forth, Hudson's fingertips trailed across Rocky's skin. The feeling of intimacy doubled. The air felt heavy with desire. No one made any moves beyond the most innocuous of touches.

With his free hand, Hudson took Jinx's hand. He toyed with Jinx's fingers. "I hate that our time is ending," Hudson said as he watched their fingers linking and stroking. Rocky was mesmerized by the sight too. He couldn't explain why. "I have a thing tonight."

"It's okay. We'll see each other again."

Even though Hudson kept his head down, Rocky still caught a quick glimpse of Hudson's smirk. "You're not even going to ask what thing I have, are you? You're not the least bit jealous or curious."

A low and sexy-sounding chuckle rumbled from Jinx. "First off, it's not my business. If you wanted to tell me, you would. Second, I have no right to be jealous. You belong to the world first and not at all to me."

Hudson's chin lifted. "That's not true." His green eyes looked earnest in a way that Rocky had never seen him look before. "Do you remember when you asked me what it's like being me, and I said I felt like I'm always skating a super fine line?"

"Yes."

At Jinx's response, a sad smile passed over Hudson's lips. Rocky found himself engrossed in the conversation. Hudson's gaze moved between them. He almost seemed shy in that moment. "I didn't feel that way today."

Rocky didn't know what Hudson was talking about since he hadn't been present for the conversation referenced. He got the gist of it, though. Today, Hudson had gotten to be normal. Rocky imagined that didn't happen often. Working for Zayn had given Rocky some insight into the rich and famous. It was a lonely existence. Rocky couldn't let Hudson be alone. "You should hang out with us more often, then."

Hudson smiled. His spine melted against the door and his palm smoothed down Rocky's arm as he went. "I'd like that. Things have been kind of crazy lately. I dropped two albums back-to-back right after coming off tour. Now I have a small role in an upcoming movie. That's what I'm doing tonight. We're filming my scenes."

"That sounds... legitimately exhausting," Jinx said, mirroring Rocky's thoughts. No doubt, Jinx knew better than him. As the sound man for Spencer's alter ego, Zealous Blaze, he understood the hard work it took for just one show, much less an entire tour and everything else Hudson listed.

Hudson stared at nothing while playing with Jinx's fingers. "I've been tired a long damn time."

. . .

Even though Hudson sounded distant, Rocky's chest tightened. There was something in his tone. It spoke to Rocky and scared him a little. He didn't know why he felt so close to Hudson after one afternoon together. Something was happening between the three of them. Maybe they had merely uncovered a deep kinship. No matter the reason for his feelings, Rocky didn't want him to be sad.

"Call us when you're done." The words were out there before Rocky could think them through.

Hudson's gaze collided with Rocky's and didn't budge. He looked as if he held his breath. For a moment, no one spoke. Then Hudson gave the subtlest of nods. Air filled Rocky's lungs, making him realize he had been the one holding his breath. Jinx squeezed his knee but didn't look his way. Rocky wondered what he had started. He wasn't sure, but one thing was crystal clear. There was no going back.

TWO

LIGHTS TWINKLED in the night sky for as far as the eye could see. Wind ruffled Hudson's hair and made goosebumps rise on his skin. He tried keeping his mind blank. Nothing good ever came from his thoughts anymore. Instead, he focused on the city lights. His mood had taken a downhill turn immediately after filming wrapped. Some people he had never met invited him to dinner. Another random dude offered to blow him in the bathroom while simultaneously doing a hit of coke. No one blinked an eye. While most days he never stopped to think about how fucked up everyone was around him, tonight he noticed. Sometimes, from seemingly out of nowhere, it would hit Hudson. His entire life had been exactly like this. Since he was thirteen, grown men he didn't even know had calmly offered to keep him serviced in every way. Fake smiles and greedy glances always flashed his way. Now, at thirty-one, Hudson was a complete mess. He had never stood a chance.

Before tonight, the day had been a good one. It had started out iffy. He had gone to lunch with some random guys, feeling self-destructive as hell. Hudson had thought to spend the day immersing himself in every sin. Then Jinx had saved him. A smile tugged at the corners of Hudson's mouth. *Jinx...* Hudson took a cleansing breath. They had met a few years back when Hudson hired Zealous Blaze to DJ a party out in the desert. From their first conversation, Hudson had known Jinx was different—like his brain didn't work the same as everyone else's in the world. Jinx didn't pretend to like things if he didn't. He didn't smile if he didn't feel it. It was like Jinx's brain was extremely linear. He didn't stray from the path of good and right. Jinx was honest and sweet. Untainted. He let Hudson touch him because he liked Hudson as a person. That was exactly why

Hudson should stay away from him. Jinx liked the parts of Hudson that Hudson had shown him. There was an ugly side no one should see.

Hudson dropped his gaze to the pool three stories below. He had this beautiful home and gorgeous cars. There was nothing he couldn't buy; except he didn't think he could buy Jinx. Jinx's light blue eyes flashed through Hudson's mind. The way Jinx always stared at him while hanging on every word Hudson spoke wouldn't leave Hudson's mind. A set of dark green eyes joined Jinx in Hudson's head. Rocky was opposite of Jinx in every way. He was tall. Jinx was short. He was muscular. Jinx was tiny. Rocky was older than Hudson. Jinx was younger. Whereas Jinx would never question Hudson's sanity or loyalty, Rocky would likely demand Hudson's bared soul. After spending the entire day with the pair, Hudson had never been more torn. He wasn't confused about which one he preferred or wanted the most. Hudson wanted them both. The problem was he longed to be crushed between their equal yet opposite personalities, but Hudson hated the idea of destroying them. He didn't think they realized how they looked at each other. There was so much unspoken love between them. Hudson was a leech. He would take all of that for himself, leaving them empty.

Another breeze stroked Hudson's skin. Without thought, he grabbed the railing and pushed, heaving himself up onto one of the concrete pillars that separated the tempered glass panes of his balcony. The foot-wide square surface was barely enough space for Hudson to stand on. His legs shook as he straightened. The wind felt stronger from this vantage point. His pool seemed even farther down. If he fell, the water might cushion the blow and save him, but Hudson doubted it. Hudson stretched his arms out wide and tilted his chin to the sky. He would let the gods decide. They could use a gust of wind to take him away or he could fall backward. It would hurt, but he would live. Hudson closed his eyes, accepting either fate. His heart raced into his throat as the world suddenly shifted and he flew through the air before landing roughly over a solid shoulder. The blow to his midsection knocked the air from his lungs.

· · ·

"What the actual fuck, Hudson? Have you lost your goddamn mind?" Tito stormed through the house, berating him every step. "I'm one person. Can you not act a damn fool for one fucking second so I can have a break?"

Guilt washed over Hudson. He was a terrible person.

Tito stamped down three flights of steps, making sure Hudson was jarred every step of the way. Hudson knew the move was purposeful since he had an elevator. "I'm done with it tonight. It's been a long day. As far as I'm concerned, you need to be someone else's problem so I can get some goddamn well-earned sleep." Tito stormed outside.

"I'm sorry."

Tito unlocked the SUV and opened the back door. He tossed Hudson inside. "Shut the fuck up."

· · ·

Hudson caught a glimpse of Tito's enraged expression before he slammed the door closed in Hudson's face. Hudson watched in horror as Tito stormed around the vehicle and climbed behind the wheel. A hint of panic set in. It was possible Tito had completely had enough. Maybe he would finally have Hudson locked up for being crazy.

"Where are we going?"

Tito started the vehicle. The doors automatically locked as he shifted into Drive. "I told you to shut the fuck up. You've got nothing to say I want to hear." Tito fell into an under-his-breath tirade as he drove. Hudson only caught bits and pieces of it. There was something about there being almost seven billion people in the world who would kill to have as much as Hudson, but no. Hudson had to be the ungrateful asshole blessed with everything. Hudson was mesmerized by Tito's rage. He knew Tito had put up with a lot in the decade he had worked for Hudson, but still. Before Hudson grasped where they were headed, they had arrived at their destination. Tito slammed on the brakes and was out of the car in an instant. Hudson's door flew open, and once again, Hudson was over his shoulder, fighting to breathe.

Light spilled from an open doorway. A familiar caustic-sounding voice greeted them. "Come on. This way."

Hudson tried pushing himself out of Tito's arms to explain and plead his case with Rocky. Tito smacked his ass so hard, it took Hudson's breath. The world flew past him as Tito tossed him through the air. He landed with a bounce on a soft surface. Jinx looked every bit as surprised to see Hudson as Hudson was to find himself in Jinx's bed.

"There, you selfish bastard. Explain to that one what you did." Tito stormed away. Rocky followed him out. Hudson had a bad feeling Rocky was about to get an earful from Tito, and Hudson would spend the entire night being lectured by a new set of people.

· · ·

Jinx set the book he had obviously been reading aside. He turned sideways on the bed and leaned back against the wall. It was obvious Jinx had been sitting in bed and relaxing before Hudson had been tossed into his life. He only wore a pair of thin workout shorts and nothing else.

"Hey beautiful."

Jinx smiled at the compliment. "What did you do to piss off Tito?"

"I climbed a balcony."

Jinx's smile grew. "That doesn't seem so bad."

"I was three floors up at the time."

Jinx's smile fell. He eyed Hudson in a way that immediately slowed his heart rate and lowered his blood pressure. There was something special about Jinx. He was soothing. Hudson didn't feel judged.

"Do you want to tell me what's going on?"

Hudson crossed his ankles and settled deeper into Jinx's pillows. Now that he was here, Hudson didn't want to be anywhere else. "I have green hair."

Jinx's face screwed up in confusion. "You always have brightly colored hair. What does that matter?"

A smile snapped to Hudson's lips. "Don't you know? Green hair is always the final stage of a mental breakdown."

To his surprise, Jinx reached out and took Hudson's hand. "Are you still on your meds?"

. . .

Hudson nodded. As Hudson looked on, Jinx toyed with his fingers. He kept his sexy light blue eyes locked on their joined hands. Hudson's chest filled with an unnamed emotion. Jinx's shoulders expanded and fell. It was obvious he still tried absorbing everything. He saw the ugly in Hudson. There was no going back.

Finally, Jinx's gaze met his again. "You'll stay here with me. I'll take care of you."

"You tried to jump from the balcony," Rocky roared, coming through the bedroom door.

Hudson winced. "I didn't plan to jump."

Rocky stood, looming over Hudson with his hands on his hips. "What was your plan?"

Hudson shrugged. "To let the gods decide if I lived or died." It hit him. They had decided.

. . .

With an eye roll, Rocky climbed onto the bed and sat cross-legged on the opposite side of Hudson, facing Jinx. "You're an idiot."

"So they tell me," Hudson said, unfazed. There was nothing Rocky could say Hudson hadn't heard before.

"Are you on drugs?"

It was Hudson's turn to roll his eyes at Rocky's question.

Jinx came to his rescue. "Hudson doesn't even drink, much less do drugs. He's unhappy."

"I'd be unhappy too if I didn't as much as drink," Rocky muttered under his breath, but he stroked Hudson's stomach.

. . .

The backs of Hudson's eyes burned. Tito had brought him to the right place. Hudson was fairly certain these were his only friends. He wished he wasn't a mess. They deserved better. Hudson didn't want to show any weakness. He needed to change the tone. "Have you two even kissed yet?"

The pair focused on him with an unnatural intensity, as if they fought not to look at each other.

"Don't change the subject," Rocky said at the same time as Jinx said, "No."

Hudson glanced between them. "Why? You obviously want each other." He pointed at Jinx. "You always look at him," Hudson said, moving his finger Rocky's way, "when he's not looking, and you always look his way," Hudson went back to pointing at Jinx, "when he's not looking at you. So what's the deal?" No one answered. Hudson decided he knew best. "Kiss."

. . .

"Hudson, I don't think—"

"No back talk," Hudson said, interrupting Jinx. "I want you two to kiss. This has gone on too long."

Rocky took an audible breath. "If we kiss, will you talk to us?"

Hudson didn't need to think about it. If they finally kissed, there would be no talking. "Sure."

Jinx shifted to his knees. "Fine." He leaned across Hudson like he fully intended to quickly press his lips to Rocky's and move away. The most intense longing Hudson had ever witnessed crossed Rocky's features. The moment Jinx was within striking distance, Rocky's hand shot out. He buried his fingers in Jinx's hair and hauled him forward. Rocky held tight as he delved deep. Hudson's body stirred as he watched the pair. It was just a kiss, but it was like watching the hottest sex imaginable. The desire blasting from the pair was almost tangible. Hudson took a breath and soaked up their love. For reasons he couldn't explain, Hudson felt a little better about life. Even if their love didn't extend to him, they made him feel something. He wasn't dead yet. There was something good left in the world.

Flames of desire licked at Jinx's skin. He had known Rocky would be like this. That was exactly why he had planned to steal a fast kiss and move away. Jinx wasn't sure how to feel. He didn't know why Hudson wanted this. While Jinx had always known Hudson wouldn't fall in love with him or even want a relationship with him, they had a sexual relationship. Jinx felt at sea. His chest was too full with Rocky's tongue stroking his. The world no longer existed with Rocky's lips on Jinx's skin. Unlike with Hudson, where Jinx could force himself to understand why Hudson would never want more, Jinx didn't think he could do the same with Rocky. There was no going back.

. . .

Rocky pulled away but didn't release Jinx. For a moment, they stared at each other. Rocky looked turned on. Jinx couldn't tear his gaze away from the sight.

"See what you two have been missing? All this time, pretending—" Rocky's hand shot out, snagging Hudson's shirt and cutting off his lecture. Before Jinx understood his intentions, Rocky dragged Hudson up and forward. Jinx fought to grasp his place as Rocky reclaimed Jinx's mouth, but with Hudson as part of their kiss. Jinx wasn't one to sleep around. He had never been in this position before. All he knew any longer was pure need. Until he ended up right here, Jinx hadn't realized how much he wanted it. Lately, he had been depressingly torn. His mind had been a mess. He was in love with Rocky, even though he knew it would lead to heartbreak. Jinx also hadn't protected his heart from Hudson, even though he knew Hudson only wanted to fuck him. Jinx had never felt more vulnerable than he did in that moment. He was overwhelmed. Without thought, he blindly climbed from the bed. Hands tried to keep him from leaving. Jinx didn't stop. He headed for the bathroom and into the walk-in closet where he had found a secret passageway a few months back. Once inside the quiet passageway inside the walls, Jinx finally stopped and took a breath. With his eyes closed, he leaned against the wall and focused on the sound of the air leaving his lungs. Humiliation tried creeping in, but Jinx shut his mind against it. No one understood. It had been less than a year since his mom died and his life changed. Zayn had taken him in and saved his sanity, but Jinx still wasn't whole. He didn't have the strength to get his heart broken. Hudson and Rocky were probably fucking in Jinx's bed right now and... goddamn it. Jinx just wanted to be special to someone. Why wasn't he special? His eyes burned. He couldn't stop the tears from falling. Jinx covered his face. He tried breathing through the pain, but the tears wouldn't stop. There was no strength left in him after years of watching his mom wither away. He was tired, and he missed having someone love him unconditionally. Jinx couldn't carry this. He might not survive the fall.

"I'm sorry."

. . .

Jinx wasn't surprised Rocky found him. He swiped at his eyes. "Fuck. Don't apologize. That makes it worse."

Rocky didn't say anything else. Jinx still couldn't look his way. He felt like an idiot.

"I'm guessing you've changed your mind about me staying with you."

Fuck his life. Hudson was here too. It seemed everyone would get to witness him falling apart. "Could you both just go away?"

"No."

A watery-sounding laugh burst from Jinx at Rocky's answer. He swiped harder at his eyes, trying to make the tears stop. "Surprise. I'm a mess. Does it make you feel better to see it?"

· · ·

"You're not a mess. Hudson is the disaster."

"Gee, thanks," Hudson muttered at Rocky's claim.

Rocky snorted. "Everyone knows green hair is the last stage of a mental breakdown."

A smile unexpectedly pulled at Jinx's lips. He felt like an idiot. Jinx took a calming breath. "I'm sorry."

Hudson hissed. "Damn. I see now why you didn't want an apology. Don't say that. It makes me feel like you didn't want to be kissed."

At Hudson's claim, Jinx finally found the strength to turn his head and look their way. Rocky and Hudson looked every bit as upset as Jinx. He felt like shit. They were good men. It genuinely wasn't their fault he had been at his breaking point for a long time. "I don't know what I want. That's not true," Jinx said every bit as quickly. "I'm just not very strong."

. . .

Rocky nodded—like he understood. "That's okay. How about we go to bed and I hog the covers? You two can fight for warmth and I'll know you're both safe for the night."

Jinx sniffed and straightened away from the wall. He nodded, since he didn't think his voice would work. As a unit, they headed back to Jinx's bed. Jinx climbed in and watched as Hudson and Rocky stripped down to their underwear. They were equally gorgeous, but in different ways. Even though Hudson wasn't a big guy, he was still bigger than Jinx. Jinx felt tiny while waiting for the pair to join him. He didn't know where he should be, so he stayed in the middle of his bed, where he usually slept. Hudson climbed over him and settled on one side while Rocky took the other.

"Let me be the first to tell you; you're an adult now. It's time to put your bed in the center of the room." Hudson snuggled in close as he made the suggestion. He kissed Jinx's cheek. "I'm older than you and pee a lot. You can't make me climb over everyone all night, every night like this."

"We'll fix it tomorrow," Rocky said, planning Jinx's life as he too scooted as close as possible. "You'll survive for one night."

Jinx wanted to ask how many nights they intended to spend in his bed, but he was too scared to start that subject. Instead, he stayed stiff while trying to force his muscles to relax.

Hudson stroked his stomach. "Please don't take your friendship away now. You're the only person who doesn't use me."

Jinx finally relaxed. He linked fingers with Hudson's and held on. "Please stop thinking about my stupidity. I already feel like a big enough idiot." He blew out a breath.

. . .

"You're not an idiot." Rocky sounded stern. It made butterflies stir in Jinx's stomach. "It's been a rough year. Why do you think I haven't kissed you before tonight? I wanted you to know that you can trust me. You obviously don't know it yet."

Jinx's eyes fell closed. "That's not true. I trust you completely. We should try again." Resolve settled over Jinx as he made the demand. "Kiss me again. Both of you."

Neither man moved.

"Then kiss each other and let me watch," Jinx suggested, hoping to get things moving.

For a moment, Rocky and Hudson eyed each other. Finally, Hudson came up onto his elbow and leaned over Jinx. Rocky did the same. He didn't grab Hudson and pull him into a fiery kiss the way he had Jinx, but he also didn't back down when Hudson reached for him. Jinx's breaths came a little faster as he watched Hudson's and Rocky's lips meet. His cock stirred when the kiss deepened. He never expected the lack of jealousy, much less to be turned on by the sight of Hudson and Rocky together. The bigger his desire got, the smaller his fears became. When their kiss turned heated, Jinx drew the pair down until he had Rocky's mouth and Hudson kissed his neck. He lost himself in the sensation of stroking tongues as Hudson joined their kiss and their mouths moved from one spot to another. Jinx no longer knew whose hands touched him or whose tongue was in his mouth. All he knew was lust as someone's hand found its way inside his shorts. Jinx moved against the palm that stroked him while stealing all the kisses they could give. His hands made their way beneath the covers. Lust made him bold. He rubbed the erections on either side of him until each man freed their cocks for Jinx to touch.

Jinx couldn't think straight. They were so different yet the same. While each man felt soft yet hard, that was where the similarities ended. Hudson had a dick Jinx could ride all night. He was the perfect length and width so Jinx wouldn't get hurt. Rocky's dick matched the man. It was thick and long, ensuring Jinx would stretch and gag. Jinx was so goddamn horny, he thought he might scream. He stroked and tugged while moving restlessly, seeking more. Rocky sat up and ripped Jinx's shorts off before settling down again. He roughly pulled Jinx's leg over his hip, spreading Jinx's thighs. Jinx lost himself in the sensation of Hudson sucking his nipple. Rocky sucked two fingers, wetting them before Jinx found them in his ass. His eyes rolled back in his head. Rocky pumped his fingers, massaging the perfect spot while Hudson tugged on Jinx's dick. Jinx blindly stroked, taking whatever kisses he could from whoever gave them. His hips rolled as he tried reaching for release. Everything felt too good. He wanted more, yet he needed this to end. Pressure climbed his shaft. Jinx strained toward it. As a loud gasp ripped from his throat, an orgasm nearly blinded him. Neither Rocky nor Hudson stopped. They kept tormenting Jinx until he had nothing left to give. Then both men shot to their knees and openly jacked off while Jinx fought for air. Grunts and moans filled the air. Hot cum coated Jinx's torso as they came all over him. In all his life, Jinx had never felt more complete. It was as if everything snapped into place. Jinx wanted them both. He might not get to keep them, but in this moment, they were his. Jinx couldn't ask for more.

THREE

THERE WAS a weird pressure in Rocky's chest after watching Jinx and Hudson sleep for half the night. There was also a huge weight sitting on his shoulders. Despite a bit of sexual gratification, everyone was miserable, and he didn't know how to fix it. It took Rocky a moment to realize Hudson's eyes were open. Light spilling from the cracked bathroom door was enough for Rocky to see him clearly. For a long moment, they silently stared at each other across Jinx's sleeping form.

Finally, Rocky broke. "Why did you try jumping from the balcony?"

. . .

51

Hudson looked away and stared at Jinx. "You wouldn't understand."

Rocky fought an eye roll. "Being unhappy isn't a problem owned only by the rich and famous."

Rocky didn't think Hudson would answer. Since their whispering would likely wake Jinx soon, he considered letting go. "I thought being an adult would be different," Hudson admitted finally, surprising Rocky. "Like I thought I would wake up one day and magically have my shit together." Hudson's gaze moved back Rocky's way. "He kisses me all the time and doesn't freak out."

Rocky knew this answer without having to think about it. "That's because he trusts you. He doesn't trust me." It hurt to admit that, but it was the truth.

Hudson shook his head. "It's because he's not scared to lose me. I'm nobody to him. He's terrified of losing you. It's like I'm not a real person to anyone. Maybe not even to me."

"I feel sick at the thought of losing either of you," Jinx whispered, proving he had been awake for at least part of their conversation.

Rocky winced. "I'm sorry. I didn't mean to wake you."

Jinx opened one eye. "You're holding a conversation across my face. I'm a deep sleeper but not that deep."

The moment felt intimate, disclosing secrets in the dark. Rocky had confessions he needed to make too. "I don't know what I want from this."

"I don't expect anything," Hudson said immediately, sounding hurt and obviously misunderstanding.

· · ·

Rocky couldn't let that go on. "I don't think I'm very good at expressing myself. Maybe just hear me out while I trip over my thoughts out loud." Hudson and Jinx nodded, giving Rocky hope he might make them understand. He started with Jinx. "Since the first night you stayed here, I've known that I want to be with you. I know you're still hurting from losing your mom, and I haven't known how to tell you I'm here when you're ready." Rocky switched his gaze to Hudson. "You, I wasn't expecting at all. You just kind of sideswiped me. In fact, I wanted to hate your face because it felt like you were slowly stealing Jinx from me. I have nothing to offer. To either of you," he added, looking between Jinx and Hudson. He couldn't stop there. "Honestly, I'm super confused because I've never been happier than I am right now." Rocky's chest felt like it was caving in. "I don't think I'm explaining myself very well. I just said I don't know what I want, but I kind of do. It's just that I don't think what I want is realistic."

Jinx didn't let him flounder. "What do you want?"

. . .

Rocky didn't respond right away. He wasn't sure he was brave enough.

Hudson sat up. "I think I should go. You two have a lot to talk about."

At Hudson's threat to leave, Rocky's heart tried jumping into his throat. His confession burst from him in his panic. "I want the three of us to be together." Hudson froze. Rocky clarified his outburst so there would be no misunderstanding. "As like a throuple or whatever. Jesus, you two are being really quiet and I'm just out here, rambling like an idiot."

"I want that too," Jinx said, saving him. "Honestly, I've wanted that for a while. I just haven't been strong enough to admit it, and I'm kind of a mess and no one's catch." Jinx stroked Hudson's chest and Hudson settled back down. As Rocky looked on, Jinx traced the line of Hudson's jaw with his fingertip. "You probably don't care to be tied down, and I get it. I've tried really hard not to get attached. You've never done anything to lead me on or to make me believe you want a relationship. It's not your fault I'm greedy." Jinx took a shaky-sounding breath. "I didn't mean to fall for you while trying to hide from feeling too much for Rocky. It just happened."

Rocky thought his heart would explode. Jinx felt something for him. He had never been happier.

"You're a real person to me," Jinx whispered, saying what Rocky didn't know how to articulate. "I want you with us."

Hudson looked between them. "I have issues."

Jinx nodded. "I know."

Hudson didn't stop there. "Sometimes I leap from balconies."

. . .

A smile snapped to Rocky's lips. "We've been made aware."

"And to be fair, I cry for no reason these days, which is super unattractive, so... there's that if we're comparing weaknesses," Jinx said, making Rocky's smile grow.

Hudson's gaze softened as he stared at Jinx. "You're the realest person I know. That's no weakness."

Jinx bit his bottom lip, obviously trying to squelch a smile. "So... we should probably try that three-way kiss thing again, don't you think? We should get the hang of it."

A smile exploded across Hudson's face. "We definitely should."

Rocky didn't wait for anyone to change their mind. He dove in with every bit of enthusiasm in his heart.

Since he had never been in a relationship like this one, nor had he had much luck with any relationship at all, Rocky imagined this would likely blow up in their faces. He was willing to let it happen for a shot at hanging on to this level of happiness. Rocky needed to try.

For all Hudson's fears about having to pee a hundred times during the night, it ended up being Jinx who abandoned them first. Hudson was the first one to venture out, looking for something to drink. It was thirsty work making out with two men. Hudson couldn't stop smiling. In his distraction, he wandered into the middle of some heavy petting happening inside the kitchen.

"Whoa. Sorry. I didn't see you there." Hudson tried looking in every direction but at Zayn and Spencer. It was their house, and they had every right to do whatever, wherever.

. . .

"Hey, Hudson. I didn't know you were here." Spencer didn't sound concerned about Hudson standing in his kitchen in his underwear.

Hudson dared a glance their way. They were in their underwear too, but everything was hidden. "Yeah. Sorry. I stayed the night and just popped in here to grab some water."

Zayn smiled. "I take it you slept in Jinx's room."

"Hey, grab two more bottles and we'll take one to..." Rocky froze as he spotted Spencer and Zayn. He too wore nothing but his underwear.

Zayn's smile slipped away.

Spencer's eyebrows rose.

.   .   .

Jinx padded into the kitchen wrapped in a sheet. "Are we getting something to..."

Spencer's eyebrows somehow got higher.

Zayn's expression snapped closed.

Everyone looked at everyone else, as if no one dared to be the first to say anything. Rocky looked a bit pale, and it occurred to Hudson he might be jeopardizing Rocky's job.

"I got your wedding invitation," Hudson said to break the tension. "Consider me RSVP'd."

A smile exploded across Spencer's face. He looked away, as if trying to hide it.

Zayn looked as if he'd run through a list of responses in his head before choosing to attack things head on.

"So, are the three of you..." It was obvious he didn't know how to finish that question.

"Yes," Hudson, Rocky, and Jinx said simultaneously. They shared a smile.

"Okay." Zayn straightened away from the counter where Spencer had him pinned only moments ago. "We were just headed back to bed. If you're all still around in a few hours, maybe we can have breakfast together."

"Sounds great," Jinx answered for them. "We're in my room, if you're ready and don't see us."

With a nod, Spencer linked fingers with Zayn and disappeared through a hidden panel in the kitchen. The moment they were gone, Rocky covered his face with both hands.

. . .

Jinx rushed to soothe him. He rubbed Rocky's back. "Don't worry. I've known Spencer a long time. He won't care about this."

"Also, I won't let you be homeless if this ends up becoming an issue," Hudson added, because he would not let anyone toss Rocky into the street.

Rocky dropped his hands. He looked defeated. "Sorry. Even though Zayn and I haven't really had the normal boss and employee relationship over the years, that was still brutal. He gave me a job when he could've had my ass tossed in jail." Rocky scrubbed his fingers through his hair. Hudson's thoughts scattered as he watched Rocky's muscles flex.

Jinx looked every bit as fascinated.

Hudson tried pulling his thoughts back on track. "Like I said, I won't let this relationship hurt you. I don't think Spencer or Zayn seemed bothered, but if you find out differently, you can come live with me.

BEAUTIFULLY TORN

My house isn't quite this massive, and I don't have any secret passageways, but you'd be comfortable."

Rocky chuckled. His sexy green eyes flashed with humor. "Did you see their faces?" He snorted. "I think we shocked them a little."

Jinx walked around them and opened the fridge. "Considering they are absolute freaks, I don't think we have to worry about any judgment from that pair." Jinx pulled three bottles of water from the fridge before turning back their way. "But I still imagine we should be prepared to get side-eyed by some people. Are you two ready to go back to bed?"

Hudson was so fucking proud of how calm Jinx sounded because he was right. There would be some people who judged them. Right now, though, there was nothing Hudson wanted more than to go back to bed.

It was a tiny bit possible Jinx was nowhere near as calm on the inside as he pretended to be. The thing was, though, he was too happy to let that fear ruin what they were starting. He swore he felt Rocky's and Hudson's hungry stares following him to the bedroom. Jinx expected they would pounce any second. He couldn't wait.

Inside the bedroom, Jinx set his water aside, tossed the sheet back onto the bed, and calmly climbed back into bed. Since he was nude, he might have made a bit of a show of it, but he could still feel their eyes. When he settled onto his back, Jinx fought a smile. Hudson and Rocky were staring at him like starving wolves. Side by side, they peeled their underwear off, letting their erections spring free. Jinx's hand automatically went for his cock. It hardened as his fingers encircled his shaft. He stroked as he eyed the men that he hoped would soon be inside him. Jinx didn't care which one fucked him as long as someone did. He felt empty.

. . .

Hudson climbed over him, licking Jinx's crown as he went. Jinx's eyes fell closed. His skin felt like it was too tight. He needed release.

"Please tell me you have condoms in here."

Jinx stared at Rocky's huge cock as he responded. "I'm sorry. I don't. There has to be some somewhere in this house." Damn. He hoped so because Jinx wanted that dick.

Rocky stroked himself, making Jinx's hunger grow. Hudson kissed Jinx's neck. Jinx's hips automatically rolled.

Rocky's eyes seemed to glaze over while watching them. "Um. Damn. Give me a minute. I'll cut through the walls to my bedroom and grab what we need." Rocky disappeared in a hurry.

. . .

Jinx might have laughed at his enthusiasm if he wasn't so goddamn turned on. He needed Rocky to get back as fast as possible.

Hudson hovered over Jinx, stealing kisses. He pulled away just enough to hold Jinx's stare. "Are you sure about this? I don't want you to resent me."

Without thought, Jinx's finger slid up the bridge of Hudson's nose. From there, he traced one of Hudson's perfectly shaped eyebrows. He was such a beautiful man. "I can't tell you how much you live in my thoughts. Why are you so flawless?"

"I can afford to be."

A smile pulled at Jinx's lips as he stroked Hudson's nose again before lightly fingering Hudson's lip piercing. "I don't mean on the outside, even though you are incredibly hot. It's your heart. You're so beautiful on the inside, I knew right away one time with you would never be enough." Jinx pushed at

Hudson's chest, urging him onto his back. He kissed the lip ring he had been toying with. Hudson had a lot of sexy piercings. There were a few in places meant to bring the most pleasure. Jinx kissed Hudson's chin before moving lower. He licked Hudson's pierced nipples. "Damn. I miss you when you're too busy for me."

Jinx slithered lower, tonguing Hudson's ribs, counting each one on the way down. "Do you ever think about me?"

"All the goddamn time." Hudson sounded breathless. Jinx hoped to make it worse.

He licked Hudson's crown, teasing him by toying with his Prince Albert piercing. Hudson moaned and Jinx took Hudson's length. As his lips closed around Hudson's cock, Hudson's body bowed like he had never felt anything better. Warm lips touched the small of Jinx's back as the bed dipped beside them. Jinx's eyes rolled back in pleasure.

. . .

"You two are so damn sexy together." Wet fingers probed at Jinx's ass. "Fuck. You have no idea how many nights I've jacked off while imagining pushing my way inside this tight asshole."

Between the taste of Hudson's cock, Hudson acting like he was getting the blow job of a lifetime, and Rocky's words, Jinx was already ready to explode. He was mindless on Hudson's dick, giving him everything.

Rocky spread Jinx's ass cheeks wide. "Mhmm. Look at that greedy hole, begging for me. You are everything I want." Rocky's wide crown pushed against Jinx's asshole. Jinx sucked in a ragged breath around Hudson's cock. While Jinx owned some big toys, Rocky was bigger than Jinx usually took. Luckily, he was too horny and distracted to tense. Rocky took advantage and thrust. A cry tore from Jinx as Rocky's dick punched his prostate at just the right spot and angle. He had never come so hard and fast in his life. Jinx sucked and bobbed on Hudson's cock, going wild as Rocky ruined him for anyone else.

. . .

"Oh, fuck. Goddamn. I've never... holy shit." A loud cry vibrated against his spine as Rocky bit his back.

Hudson grabbed Jinx's hair and pulled. "Suck it. Yes. You're fucking amazing. Yes." A guttural-sounding groan assaulted Jinx's ears as hot cum filled his mouth. Jinx let the mixture of cum and saliva roll down Hudson's cock as he pumped at Hudson's shaft, finishing him. Hudson's muscles relaxed like he turned to gelatin beneath Jinx. He panted like he had run a marathon.

Rocky's fingers encircled Jinx's jaw. He pulled Jinx up and back, twisting until he could claim Jinx's mouth—like he hunted for Hudson's cum.

Jinx could barely cling to a single thought as they collapsed into a heap of sweaty bodies in Jinx's bed. They kissed and petted one another. Time passed as they lingered in the passion of the moment. At some point, Rocky cleaned them—like the caretaker he was. When Jinx finally drifted off to sleep, a smile still lingered on his lips. For the first time in ages, he was truly happy. It was possible it was only for one night. They might wake up in a few hours and realize this wouldn't work. For now, Jinx was at peace. They were three men looking for a loving forever home. It felt like they had found it.

FOUR

HUDSON: *I think I'll go pink with the hair today.*

Jinx: *I like pink.*

Rocky: *I could see you in pink.*

Hudson: *May I take you both to dinner tonight afterward?*

Rocky: *I'm working.*

. . .

Jinx: *Sure.*

Rocky: *You two should definitely go and have fun. I'll come to you when I get off.*

Hudson: *Damn right, you'll come.*

Rocky: *Looking forward to it.*

———

Rocky: *Where are you? I've looked everywhere.*

Jinx: *Mom wanted part of her ashes scattered on the beach. I finally worked up the strength to do it.*

Rocky: *Why didn't you wait on me? You shouldn't do that alone.*

. . .

Jinx: *I wanted to do it alone, but thank you. Will you be home when I get back?*

Rocky: *Definitely.*

Jinx: *Good. I need you.*

Rocky: *You've got me, baby.*

Jinx: *Are you home?*

Hudson: *Yep.*

Jinx: *Is it okay if I come by? Rocky is working and I'm bored.*

Hudson: *Absolutely. I'm in my studio. I'd love your help to improve some sounds.*

. . .

Jinx: *I'm always your man.*

Hudson: *Damn right, you are.*

Rocky: *How do you feel about kidnapping Jinx and the three of us going camping?*

Hudson: *Like in a tent?*

Rocky: *Yep. Old school roughing it.*

Hudson: *In the middle of nowhere?*

Rocky: *Exactly. Out where no one can hear you scream.*

. . .

Hudson: *I'm in.*

Spencer: *I expect all three of you to be here on time for the rehearsal tomorrow night.*

Hudson: *Tito knows. He's the one who keeps me on schedule, so I'll be there.*

Rocky: *Jinx and I live here, so no problem on our end.*

Jinx: *I was just typing the same thing.*

Spencer: *Good. You three are really important to us. We want you with us.*

Hudson: *Awww.*

. . .

Rocky: *You got it.*

Jinx: *We love you both and wouldn't miss it.*

While watching Jinx and Rocky stand at the altar together, side by side, standing up for their friends, Hudson felt something. They looked beautiful. The flowered arch. A man of God. Hudson fully believed Jinx and Rocky should have that. He felt a swell of pride and relief when he imagined them married.

Now that the wedding and reception were over, they were slightly drunk and hanging out in the game room. That feeling of needing Jinx and Rocky settled hadn't faded. No matter how hard Hudson tried, he couldn't stop watching Rocky and Jinx on the sly. At six-foot four, Rocky almost had a full foot on Jinx's five-foot six status. He was solid and hard-looking. Rocky rarely smiled, and his dark green eyes always held an ounce of rage. Hudson shouldn't have been intrigued by him. Rocky should have never caught his eye. God knew he was opposite of Hudson in

76

every way. But Rocky had Hudson's attention, and Hudson couldn't stop craving him. He was thankful for that.

Rocky had touched him a lot today. Hudson had been aware of every single instance. While Rocky always let Jinx and Hudson touch him as much as they dared, today, Rocky had initiated a majority of the contact. Hudson needed more. He longed for human touch. Hudson fought the urge to beg Rocky and Jinx to give him the attention he needed. After all, he had them now. For a long time, Hudson had danced around Jinx, only tasting him occasionally. Now, for four months, he'd had Rocky and Jinx. It felt like a miracle. Hudson had to find a way to keep them forever.

"You two looked perfect together at that altar today."

Jinx flashed him a smile and went back to battling Rocky in their video game. He spoke over his shoulder. "It felt good to stand up there with

Spencer. I like knowing he's settled with someone who loves him the way he deserves."

Even though neither man faced him, Hudson still nodded. "I'm sure, but that's not what I meant. You two should get married."

Rocky laughed. "Um. No. Now is probably a good time to say that I don't plan to marry. I get that we fought really hard for the right to do so, but it's not for me."

That was not what Hudson hoped to hear. It also hadn't escaped his attention that Jinx hadn't responded. "What about you, Jinx?"

Jinx kept his gaze locked on the TV. "What about me?"

Hudson fought an eye roll. "Do you see yourself as someone's husband someday?"

. . .

"I'd always hoped so, yes."

Rocky tossed a quick and uncomfortable-looking glance Jinx's way. Jinx kept his stare glued to the TV like his life depended upon it. Rocky's character died and Jinx flashed him a bright smile. "Ha. You owe me a kiss."

Rocky immediately snagged the back of Jinx's neck and claimed his mouth. Hudson watched the entire scene with two parts pride and one part sadness. It was obvious Jinx wanted something out of life that Rocky would never give. Hudson was gone a lot. He wished they could be settled.

Rocky pulled away and stood. "Well, guys. I think I'll run upstairs, grab a shower, and find something comfortable to wear. Then maybe we can find some of that leftover reception food."

. . .

Jinx nodded. "Sounds good."

Rocky gave Hudson a quick kiss before leaving them alone. Hudson watched as Jinx put away their game controllers. There was a hint of unhappiness in Jinx's features—like his shoulders sagged. Hudson couldn't take it.

"I could see you happily married. You'd make a great husband."

A small smile touched Jinx's lips. "I always kind of liked the thought of being settled. My mom used to talk about planning the perfect wedding for me. She wanted to know I would be happy after she was gone. I guess it's hard to top today's wedding, though. It was pretty perfect." Jinx released a tired-sounding breath. "Would you like to join me for a shower?"

The muscles in Hudson's stomach automatically clenched in anticipation of touching Jinx. There was nothing he loved more. "That sounds amazing.

Come here first." Even Hudson heard the hunger in his voice.

Jinx's gaze locked on Hudson. He held Hudson's stare as he crossed the room. As he reached Hudson's side, Hudson snagged Jinx's waist and towed him forward until Jinx straddled his lap. They never looked away from staring into each other's eyes. Hudson wouldn't let Jinx be sad. He couldn't. Jinx's pain made his chest ache.

"I have something to say."

Jinx nodded. "I'm listening."

Hudson took a breath. He loved the way Jinx smelled—like something sweet Hudson could eat. "It's something you already know."

"That's okay. There's nothing I'd rather be doing than listening to you telling me the same stories for the rest of our lives."

Fuck. Hudson wanted that so badly. "Good, because I love you."

Jinx went still, as if he held his breath.

Hudson wasn't finished. "I think you know I do and that I have for a long time. You also know I'm not very good at dealing with my emotions. They're there, though. I'm completely in love with you."

Jinx visibly swallowed. He looked ready to cry. When he spoke, his voice broke, proving Hudson's thoughts true. "I love you too."

Hudson urged Jinx's mouth down to his. When their lips met, Hudson's heart skipped a beat. He had known when they spent their first night together that Jinx was special. Jinx had let Hudson kiss him because he wanted to kiss. It had nothing to do with

Hudson's fame. They had come together like two men who wanted each other on a higher level. Jinx was every love song Hudson had written since. He felt all those words again as their tongues stroked.

Hudson pulled away just enough to keep whispering everything in his heart. "I swear you'll make your mom's dreams come true. If you'll still have me when all the touring is done, I'd marry you in a heartbeat."

"There's nothing you could do to drive me away. I'll be here when you're ready."

The backs of Hudson's eyes burned as he claimed Jinx's mouth once more. Before tonight, he had never once considered marriage, but he would marry Jinx one day. That was a vow. He felt in his soul that was his destiny. Hudson couldn't wait to embrace it. They were meant to be.

As hot water trailed down their bodies, Jinx immersed himself in every kiss and touch Hudson gave. The scent of shampoo, body wash, and cum filled his nostrils. He had no idea how long they lingered. Jinx couldn't move past Hudson's declaration of love. Hudson felt things deeper than other people. That was why he was always one terrible day away from stepping into traffic. Hudson was one hundred percent an Empath. Jinx believed that to the bottom of his soul. That meant Hudson loving him was something Hudson would do and feel with every fiber of his being. Jinx had never expected to be so blessed.

Hudson had already worked one orgasm from Jinx. Still, he slowly pumped inside Jinx's ass with no sign of stopping anytime soon. Hudson kept swapping between pulling Jinx back against his chest so he could steal kisses and pushing Jinx away so he could bend him over in the shower. Jinx hadn't caught his breath yet.

. . .

The shower door opened. Rocky leaned against the frame. "Damn. I came in here to tell you I had our food heated and set up, but fuck. This is hot."

Jinx watched Rocky's erection grow inside his jogging pants. His mouth watered.

"You should join us," Hudson cajoled, sounding breathless and aroused.

Rocky shook his head. "I've already showered, and I like to watch."

With no real plan, Jinx snagged the waistband of Rocky's pants and pulled him into the shower, clothes and all. Rocky laughed but didn't fight him. His laughter turned to moans when Jinx popped the erection from his pants and swallowed it. Jinx closed his eyes. He let the sensations of the moment wash over him. Jinx lost himself while Hudson fucked him, and Rocky's dick bruised his throat. He was happy. They were happy. Jinx would go as far as to say none of them had felt this level of joy before they found one another. He wanted to spend the rest of his life like this. Jinx would never admit it, but Rocky had hurt him earlier when he said he never wanted to marry. All his life, even when it hadn't been legal, Jinx had dreamed of having a happy marriage one day. It wasn't about the wedding. That didn't matter. He wanted one of those marriages he saw on the news where people were married seventy years and died holding hands. Jinx's life was already different because the three of them were together. Then Rocky had said he didn't want to be a husband. It was leveling. That one admission made Jinx question everything about them and their future.

Then Hudson had rescued him. Jinx had never dreamed Hudson would be the person who wanted to walk down the aisle with him. That new tidbit had Jinx's mind all over the place. His heart did cartwheels. He saw a future for them. One where they each got what they wanted for themselves. Jinx felt a level of peace and happiness he never had. He needed to make his men fly.

. . .

Hudson's grip turned bruising on Jinx's hips. Jinx sucked harder and faster, needing Rocky's orgasm. When it hit, Jinx found himself squished between his men. Rocky kissed him so deeply that he couldn't breathe while moaning around Jinx's tongue. Hudson's cries reverberated from the shower walls and against Jinx's shoulder. Time seemed to slow as their touch turned loving. Whispered words caressed Jinx's ears. He didn't hear a single one. Jinx's brain was filled with visions of their future. They spent every night just like this one until they were too old to do anything but hold hands. There was so much love in Jinx's chest, he thought he would explode. He had found his future. His everything.

Nothing in his life prepared Rocky to feel so much. The first twenty years of his life, Rocky had been failing at life. He hadn't been smart enough to keep up in school and had dropped out the moment he could. It was like he always set himself up to fail because he had immediately fallen in with some bad people. He was all about the fast money. The shortest path to everything. Back then, that had meant boosting cars for a quick buck. Then he had discovered Zayn's car collection. He hadn't even made it out of the driveway before he found his life turned upside down. Rocky still felt sick when he thought about how close he had been to going to prison. Instead, Zayn had saved him and put him on the road to ending up here.

Rocky stared at Jinx and Hudson. He wouldn't have met them if he hadn't started the first half of his life as a fuck-up. Sometimes, when he stopped to think about it, he was awed by life. So many tiny things had to go right for him to end up here with these men. In all his years on earth, he never dreamed he would end up in love with two men. It was strange, but then again, it wasn't. He could recall, when he was a child, his mom reading him a story. In the story, one soul had been ripped into two pieces. Those two halves spent every lifetime trying to find their way back to each other. Sometimes, souls would accidentally end up torn again, making it even harder for the pieces to find one another. Even though it had only been a story, Rocky couldn't help but think that was what happened to Hudson, Jinx, and him. That was how right they felt.

· · ·

Standing across from Jinx while Zayn and Spencer exchanged vows had fucked with Rocky's head a little. He knew he didn't want to get married. Rocky was thirty-five years old. He knew his mind. Being a husband wasn't a legal mess he wanted. But he had to admit, if he were to marry anyone, it would be Jinx. Jinx would make a great husband. He was loving and attentive. Jinx was the glue holding the three of them together. He deserved a beautiful wedding like the one they had attended today. Rocky wouldn't be the one who gave it to him. He wouldn't make a good husband. As he watched the men he loved sleep, Rocky wondered if he should get out of the way and let them have a normal life.

Rocky's chest tightened at only the thought of losing them. He couldn't do it. Maybe he was selfish, but Jinx and Hudson were his. He finally knew what it was like to be loved unconditionally. Rocky wasn't strong enough to lose them.

Jinx shifted in his sleep. Rocky pulled him into his arms, letting Jinx use his chest as a pillow. Jinx immediately settled down. Rocky had known he would. With the warmth of his men seeping into his skin, Rocky's eyes finally slipped closed. They were perfect just as they were. He had nothing to worry about. It took all three of them to be whole. Life would find a way for everything else.

FIVE

IT WAS a lot harder being on the road, knowing his heart was in L.A. Plus, it was cold as fuck in New York. Hudson had done more late-night interviews than he cared to count. He was tired and wanted to go home. Hudson had burned out so long ago, he didn't know where to start that conversation. In fact, he might not have found a way to smile through tonight's interview if the host, Tyler, hadn't pulled out Hudson's new photo album for collectors.

"Everyone is talking about this book that comes with the collector's edition of your new album."

. . .

Hudson nodded. "It was a great idea. I wish I had thought of it."

Tyler laughed along with the audience. "At least you're honest." He flipped open the book. "Everyone is talking about this image right here in particular." Tyler flashed the open pages Hudson's way before showing the audience and the camera. It was the picture of Rocky sandwiched between Hudson and Jinx. They looked amazing together. A ball of longing grew in Hudson's gut.

"Yep. Those are my guys, Jinx and Rocky."

Tyler eyed the image. "Your guys?"

Hudson nodded. "They're back in L.A., waiting for me to get home."

Tyler's eyebrows rose. "You mean the three of you are together—like in a relationship?"

. . .

"Yep. That's what I mean." Hudson wasn't embarrassed and he wouldn't start now.

Tyler smiled. It looked fake. "I imagine that's something people might find unusual."

Hudson nodded. "I'm sure, but I'm not trying to live for anyone else. Jinx and Rocky make me happy. If anyone doesn't like that, they can suck my dick. I'm not asking for permission to live my life."

The audience laughed.

Tyler's smile went through a series of transitions. One second it was fake, then real, and then pained. "Tell us a little about Jinx and Rocky."

Hudson didn't hesitate, even though he realized he should take heed. He hadn't talked to Rocky or Jinx about revealing their lives. "Jinx is sound man for Zealous Blaze and Rocky is head of security for Zayn Tanaka, so they're both successful men in their own right."

"That's amazing. Let's talk about the album that comes with this book, *Death is an Effortless Obsession*. How do Rocky and Jinx feel about the songs included?"

It was obvious Tyler was just trying to get through the interview at this point. Hudson swallowed down another wave of unhappiness. He just wanted to go home. L.A. felt farther away than ever before. The depression he always barely kept at bay pressed against his brain. It was no one's fault. Hudson had been born screwed up. Something inside him was barely attached to living. Thankfully, the moment he slid into the backseat of his hired car, Jinx's name showed up on FaceTime. Hudson couldn't answer fast enough.

"Hey, sweet baby."

. . .

Jinx smiled like he couldn't be happier to see Hudson's face. "Hi."

Rocky's face leaned into the picture. "Hey. I made it too."

"Damn." The breathless curse slipped from Hudson. His chest felt like it might cave in. He missed them that much. "I love seeing your faces."

"We watched you on the Tyler show."

At Jinx's claim, Hudson's smile wavered. "Sorry if I embarrassed you."

Rocky scowled. "Fuck that. We're always proud of you."

. . .

"Plus, we love everyone knowing you belong to us," Jinx added.

Hudson relaxed deeper into his seat. He loved staring at his men. "I miss you both so much."

"We miss you too." Rocky sounded genuine.

Hudson's chest ached. "Kiss. I want to watch."

The pair immediately did as told, making Hudson's eyes burn. Fuck. They were sexy. A voice interrupted in the background and they pulled apart.

Rocky cursed under his breath before focusing on Hudson. "I have to go. They caught someone on the property. I have to make the final call on whether the police are called. Love and miss you."

. . .

"You too." Hudson watched with his heart in his throat as Rocky stole another quick kiss and disappeared. The moment Hudson was alone with Jinx, Jinx's gaze moved over Hudson's features, as if inspecting his health.

"Why is your hair green again, baby?"

A lump formed in Hudson's throat. He tried playing it off. "I thought you liked me in green?"

"I like you in everything. Now answer my question."

"It's nothing but a hair color, sweet angel. Tell me about your day."

Jinx turned sideways on the screen, as if he settled onto his side with the phone. It was obvious he was snuggled up to his pillow. Hudson wanted to be there more than he wanted his next breath. "Well, I got up and took a shower before eating some toast.

Around one, missing you got the best of me. So I cried and then took a nap."

Hudson's heart squeezed. "You have no idea how much I wish I was there."

Jinx touched the screen, as if he could feel Hudson. "We're halfway there. You'll be home before I know it. That's what I keep telling myself."

A ragged-sounding breath escaped Hudson. "I don't know what I would do if Rocky and you weren't together. That's the only thing keeping me sane. I can't stand the thought of making you two miserable."

Jinx sighed. "You don't make us miserable. We just miss you. We knew this was part of the deal. Right now, I'm worried about you. Tell me how I can fix whatever is going on inside you."

. . .

"I love you." Hudson couldn't stop the words from bursting from him.

"I love you too."

"Make time go faster."

Jinx smiled at Hudson's demand. "I wish I could." Jinx's smile slipped away. His voice turned into a harsh whisper, as if he fought a wave of sadness. "New York is so very far away."

The car came to a stop and Tito opened the door. Hudson barely spared anyone a glance as he headed inside his hotel. He kept his eyes glued to his phone while Tito kept him safe from fans. The moment the hotel room door closed behind him, Hudson sat down on the floor and leaned his back against the door. "Do me a favor."

"Anything."

. . .

Hudson smiled at Jinx's immediate agreement. "Snuggle into your usual spot and pull the covers up."

Jinx moved to do as told. The phone moved around, giving Hudson flashes of the bedroom. He was in Rocky's bed. Longing hit Hudson like a ton of bricks.

Jinx's face reappeared on the screen. "Okay. Done."

"I'm going to tell you a bedtime story."

Jinx's smile made everything worthwhile. Hudson fell into a long, drawn out, and made-up story about a prince who fell in love with two bad boys. He revealed everything about himself in his bad-boy character. Hudson admitted to every mental failing. He droned on with no real point other than to watch Jinx fall asleep. Being away from Rocky and Jinx wasn't good for Hudson's already shaky mental health. He needed calming moments like these. Hudson would ramble for as long as it took to settle his heart. Soon enough, he would be home. Then he would never leave again.

Rocky's skin itched with irritation. He had to work, but things always went wrong at the worst times. Hudson had been gone for three months. The good and bad days came in waves. Today was a bad day. Jinx and Rocky had each other. They were enough, but they also felt Hudson missing from them all hours of the day. Jinx needed a softness that Rocky didn't have. Rocky wanted to reach through the miles and yank Hudson through space and time, dragging him back to them. It was hard as hell being powerless. All Rocky could do was watch time march on. He wanted to punch the smug kid's face who dared choose tonight to sneak onto the property. Rocky wanted to get back to Jinx and Hudson even more.

"Tonight is your lucky night. I'm feeling generous. We'll let you go with a warning."

. . .

The teen boy swept Rocky with a contemptuous gaze. "Wow. Thanks. You're so generous."

Rocky fought the urge to pinch the spot between his eyes where a pain bloomed. He hated kids, especially sarcastic ones. Instead, he tried reasoning with the arrogant shit. "You're trespassing, which is illegal."

An ugly-sounding snort escaped the ungrateful brat. "I'm a minor. Trespassing is a misdemeanor. I'll be fine."

"You'll be dead if you come back," Rocky said through clenched teeth. God. He had been just like this asshole once upon a time. Rocky wanted to kick his own ass at the thought.

"Now that's illegal," the blond shithead shot back.

. . .

Rocky shook his head and turned away. He needed to talk to Hudson. He caught the stare of one of the night guards. "Take him to a bus stop and drop him." He fought the urge to look the kid's way. "Make sure it's a stop that's too far away from here to walk back."

"Yes, sir."

Rocky headed back to the house. He hurried, but still he wasn't quick enough. It had taken him well over an hour to question the kid. Jinx was asleep. For a moment, Rocky watched him. He was such a peaceful sleeper. Love swelled in Rocky's chest. Maybe Rocky wasn't a soft person, but he loved Jinx. A lump grew in his throat. He loved Hudson too, and something wasn't right with Hudson. Rocky left Jinx behind and moved to an empty room. He pulled out his phone and called Hudson.

He answered on the second ring. "I wondered when I'd hear from you."

. . .

Hudson hadn't bothered with pleasantries. Rocky wouldn't either. "Why is your hair green again?"

"You know, Jinx and you fell in love with me with green hair. Now you're both demanding to know why I would dare go back to that color. I'm starting to wonder if your love is conditional."

Rocky rolled his eyes. "Nice dodge. Try again. What's going on?"

A long, tired-sounding breath brushed the phone and came across the miles. "I'm just exhausted, sexy. It's been a long three months and I miss my babies. That's all. I'm tired."

"Then come home. Take a break."

Silence met his suggestion and Rocky realized how unrealistic his words had been. There was never enough time from show to show to do anything other than interviews and travel. He imagined Hudson was exhausted. Rocky wanted to help.

"Are you in bed yet?"

"Headed there now." Rocky could hear the smile in Hudson's voice.

Rocky sat on the floor of the empty bedroom and leaned against the wall. "Let me know when you're tucked in." He listened as things brushed the phone.

"Okay. I'm in bed."

"Good. Close your eyes." He waited for Hudson to confirm.

"Eyes closed."

. . .

A smile tugged at the corners of Rocky's mouth. "Let me hear you take a deep breath." He listened as Hudson breathed. Rocky leaned his head back against the wall and closed his eyes. "I'm there with you, rubbing your back. Jinx is already asleep. The room is quiet."

"You're whispering you love us because you think we're asleep."

A surprised laugh burst from Rocky at Hudson's interjection. "I tell you I love you when you're awake too."

"Do you, though? I mean, you've never done a grand declaration of love or anything. Not with me and not with Jinx, as far as I've seen. You just started saying you love us one day."

"Grand declarations aren't me, baby. I try to take care of you two and tell you both I love you. Other than that, I'm not very romantic or soft." Rocky's chest tightened at the confession. He rubbed the spot that ached. He realized how lacking he was the more he spoke. "I'm sorry I'm not better at this."

"Don't apologize. You don't need to be soft. That's Jinx's job. I'm the romantic one. You have to be the one strong enough to keep us together. We each have a place, but sometimes we need to hear the words. I'm feeling pretty wiped clean right now. It's not your fault."

Rocky wanted to fix Hudson, but he didn't know how. Words escaped him in his desperation. "I love you. Being with Jinx and you, that's all I have. No one taught me how to be loving, but I can't imagine my life without you two anymore. You two are the reason I wake up."

Silence met his confession.

A soft chuckle escaped Rocky. "Did my declaration of love put you to sleep?"

. . .

"No. I was just thinking about life and our current situation. I love you too. When I get home, I'll show you just how much."

"I'll hold you to that. You need to get some sleep, baby."

Hudson's voice seemed somewhat sluggish when he responded, as if sleep already tried pulling him under. "You too. Go hold Jinx for me."

"I will. Love you and goodnight."

"Goodnight."

Rocky disconnected their call and stared at the blank wall across from him. There was definitely something going on with Hudson. Rocky wondered if Hudson had ever gone to therapy or if he was mostly just dark-natured. Not everyone was a ray of sunshine. Some people were cloudy days. The world needed both.

With no answer for anything, Rocky stood and headed back to his bedroom. He found Jinx still sleeping peacefully. Rocky stripped and joined Jinx in bed. The moment his head hit the pillow, Jinx snuggled closer, as if looking for Rocky's warmth. Rocky towed Jinx into his arms. For a long time, he stared at the ceiling and held the other piece of his heart. A smile exploded across Rocky's face from nowhere. It made sense he would fall for men who needed him. He was self-aware enough to know he thrived on being a caretaker. Rocky had watched over Zayn for fifteen years. He had built his life and personality around being strong. He loved the universe's choice for him. If given a different path in life, he would still pick Jinx and Rocky in every scenario. He was so ready for them to be together again.

SIX

HUDSON: *Are you alone?*

Jinx: *Yes.*

Hudson: *Is it okay if I call you?*

Jinx: *Of course. I'm not busy and I love hearing your voice.*

The phone rang half a second after Jinx hit send, as if Hudson had been poised with his finger over the call button. Jinx couldn't answer fast enough to suit his heart.

"Hello?"

"Hey, sexy baby. What are you wearing?"

Jinx couldn't control his smile. The happiness was too much. "Nothing."

Hudson whimpered. "I'm not alone. Why do you torment me?"

A chuckle rose in Jinx's throat. "I'm sorry, baby. I love you and couldn't resist. What's up?"

"I've been thinking a lot and missing you even more. There's a thought I'd like to run by you."

. . .

"Shoot." Jinx was more than happy to work through anything with Hudson.

"Do you think Rocky would be willing to move in with us?"

Another smile exploded across Jinx's face. "Us?"

"Yeah. Us," Hudson said without missing a beat. "My thought was that you could move in first, in secret—like Wednesday when I get home. Then we could tag team Rocky to convince him to move in too. I don't think he would move if I just asked, but I want you both with me full time when I get home."

Honestly, Jinx didn't think Rocky would move either. Rocky's home was with Zayn. It would take a lot to budge him. "Are you sure you want me full time? That's a big leap from barely seeing me in the past six months."

. . .

Hudson didn't as much as hesitate. "The idea of having the two of you in my bed every night and under my roof every day, that's all that's kept me sane. I'm ready to be happy again."

Hearing Hudson say he wasn't happy now had Jinx's heart aching.

"I love you so much. There's no place I'd rather be every night than in your bed." Jinx had to massage his chest as he said the words. Being in Hudson's bed every night might mean leaving Rocky's. Jinx equally loved both men. He didn't want to choose. "We'll convince Rocky." They had to. Jinx couldn't let Rocky say no.

"Yes. Thank you. I'm so excited." Jinx heard the excitement in Hudson's voice. Hudson kept talking like a kid high on sugar. "I love you, baby. You'll be the happiest man alive with me. I swear it. I plan to spoil you so much. You'll beg me to stop."

. . .

Jinx laughed at the idea. "Will I? I don't know. I've never been spoiled. Obviously, I have a lot of nice stuff because I live with Zayn, but I know it's not mine. I never forget I'm a guest."

"You won't be just a guest here," Hudson said, sounding firm. "Everything that's mine is yours. We're getting married someday, right?"

"Right."

Hudson released a happy sounding sigh. "Damn. I can't wait to be home with you."

Jinx closed his eyes and wished time away. "I'm so ready for you to be here. It feels like you've been gone forever." Jinx heard someone talking in the background.

. . .

Hudson groaned. "I'm sorry, baby. I have to go. A car is waiting to take me to my next show. I love you. Go snuggle with Rocky so I can picture you two happy."

"I will. I love you too. See you soon."

"Bye."

Hudson was gone again. Jinx didn't know how to feel. On one hand, he was days away from the next chapter of his life. That was exciting as hell. On the other, there was a real chance Rocky wouldn't join them. He was too entrenched here with Zayn. All Jinx could do was hope and go find Rocky like he said he would. Jinx set his phone aside and went on the hunt. He had some low-key hints to drop. There was no time like now to start.

With his paperwork balanced on one knee, Rocky worked on the next week's schedule. He needed to be off this Wednesday and possibly Thursday so he could enjoy Hudson coming home. Two guys had quit recently. One had moved for his wife's job. The other had retired, so technically, he hadn't quit. Rocky was down two people nonetheless. He would have to pull some double shifts to fill the spots until he hired some new people. That was no big deal since he lived here. It was only an inconvenience because Hudson was coming home. Rocky wanted to be there for that.

Jinx's hand ran across the back of Rocky's neck. Rocky's breath caught. His eyes fell closed. He could pick Jinx from a crowd of a thousand people without ever seeing his face. Jinx made his heart beat faster just by being in the same room.

The paperwork disappeared from Rocky's knee. Jinx pushed until he straddled Rocky's lap. Rocky drew a steadying breath as he stared into the light blue eyes that he loved more than anything.

"Hey, sweet angel. What are you doing with your day?"

. . .

Jinx stared at Rocky's mouth as he answered. "Resenting your work. It's keeping you from me."

Rocky grabbed Jinx's ass and towed him even closer. "I'm not working on anything that can't wait."

Jinx kissed Rocky's chin. "Good. We only have a few days left alone before we're at Hudson's every night. I know I'll still get to seduce you, but..." he kissed the corner of Rocky's mouth, "this is last time I'll be doing it alone."

Fuck. Rocky was torn. He had to work. Also, he couldn't wait for his men to seduce him at the same time. Not to mention, he really, really loved it when Jinx initiated things. Jinx made Rocky feel wanted, like no one else ever had. Rocky couldn't explain it. He had fucked a lot of good-looking men over the years. Jinx was special. Not only was he incredibly sexy, but he also owned Rocky's heart. No one could say that before Jinx.

. . .

Jinx coaxed him into a kiss. It wasn't until their tongues brushed that Jinx's words sank in. He pulled away. "We won't be at Hudson's every night. He usually stays here."

His pants loosened. Jinx seemed to barely listen. "He'll have a lot to catch up with at home when he gets back. I can't imagine he'll stay here for a while." Jinx went back to kissing Rocky before Rocky could respond. Then he forgot their conversation. Jinx set Rocky's erection free and stroked. Rocky's head spun. They were in Rocky's private living room, but it was still open to his employees. Everyone knew where he was in case they needed him. Anyone could walk in any second. Rocky couldn't make Jinx stop. He didn't have the strength.

Rocky moved against Jinx's hand, taking his pleasure. Jinx sucked Rocky's tongue while pumping faster. A pant escaped Rocky as he moved closer to blowing in Jinx's hand.

. . .

"Hey, Rocky. We snagged that same teenager on the property that we caught a few months back. What do you want us to do with him?"

Jinx froze.

They stared at each other.

Rocky doubted, from the angle of the doorway, Sam could see what they were doing exactly. He had definitely seen them making out, at the very least. Rocky cleared his throat and tried to sound normal. "Go ahead and call the police. I'll be out there in a minute."

"Sure thing."

Sam disappeared, and Jinx fell forward, burying his face against Rocky's throat. He shook with silent laughter. Rocky's dick was still in his hand.

· · ·

Adrenaline pumped through Rocky's veins. He couldn't believe they had been caught and he would have to face his team afterward. Sam might not say anything. Hell, he might not have seen anything since he hadn't acted as if he had. Still, they had been caught. It was kind of hot. Rocky grabbed two handfuls of Jinx's ass and stood, leaving Jinx no other choice than to wrap his legs around Rocky's waist.

"You'll pay for that one."

Jinx's eyes swam with laughter. "Is that so?"

Rocky headed inside his bedroom. "Yep. I'm about to fuck you hard and fast because I have to deal with the police. But I promise I'll come back and make love to you like you deserve later."

"I'll take it."

. . .

Rocky tossed Jinx on the bed and tore at his clothes. "Yes, you will."

Jinx moved every bit as quickly as Rocky, proving he was every bit as turned on as Rocky. In no time, Rocky was suited up, lubed, and inside Jinx. Their mouths clashed. Rocky's heartbeat pounded in his ears. Whimpers and harsh breaths filled the room. Rocky held Jinx's jaw in a tight grip, forcing Jinx to hold his stare while Rocky fucked him. "You're mine."

"I know."

At Jinx's words, Rocky blew. He came faster than he had in years. Being with Jinx, even in the quickest of trysts, was everything to Rocky. He was in love. There was nothing he wouldn't do—no low too low—to be with Jinx. He couldn't leave his baby hanging. While still trying to catch his breath from his mind-blowing orgasm, Rocky slithered down Jinx's body and swallowed his cock. The cry that tore from Jinx's throat as Rocky's lips closed around his cock was like music to Rocky's ears. He wanted to stay here all night. Rocky swore he would be back the moment he was done working.

Jinx pulled his hair and rode his tongue. He was wild beneath Rocky. As cum filled his mouth, Jinx cried his name. Rocky swallowed every drop as his prize. He was completely over-the-top enamored. Rocky would be until the day he died.

No one regretted him having to leave more than Rocky. He kissed his way back to Jinx's mouth, whispering his regrets. "I don't want to go."

Jinx kissed him deep before forcing him away. "I know. Go, so you can hurry back. I want to hold you."

A groan tore from Rocky as he moved away. He tossed the condom in the trash before righting his clothes. A whimper escaped him as he watched Jinx stretch. "Are you trying to kill me?"

. . .

A sexy smile stretched Jinx's lips. "Nope. Just trying to motivate you to come back sooner."

Rocky stared down at Jinx, debating whether he actually needed to deal with the police. Surely someone else could do it. His mind warred with itself. In the end, it was his job. He couldn't leave this big of a decision to anyone else.

"I'll hurry." Rocky raced from the room. He had to get back as fast as possible. Luckily, the police were already waiting for him by the time he reached the security office. Rocky spotted the same dirty kid he had booted from the property months earlier. He was in handcuffs and staring at the floor.

A blond cop stepped into Rocky's path before he made it inside the office. "You're Rocky Valdes, correct?"

. . .

Rocky nodded. "That's me."

The cop handed him a clipboard. "All you have to do is sign the paperwork, stating you're filing charges, and we'll take him off your hands."

Rocky eyed the paperwork. "I hate to do this, but he keeps coming back. At least he's a minor. I doubt he'll get any time."

"Actually, he's eighteen. He'll likely get a year."

A groan escaped Rocky before he could call it back. He eyed the kid sitting inside the office. He tapped the pen on the clipboard. If he signed, he could ruin the guy's life. It looked like he already had enough problems. "Do you know his deal?"

The cop glanced toward the office before meeting Rocky's stare again. "Yeah. We pick up Cooper about once a week. Usually, it's just to make him move. People don't like him sleeping on their property. Big places like this are a better choice for some of the homeless, especially teens. He's less likely to get caught or molested. It's likely he's slept in your yard several times, and that's why he keeps coming back. That, or someone on the staff is feeding him."

Rocky took a slow, steady breath. "Fuck." He handed the clipboard back to the cop. "I'm not pressing charges. We'll deal with him."

"Whatever you want. If you change your mind, just give us a call."

It wasn't a matter of changing his mind. Rocky already didn't want to deal with this, but he couldn't go back to his warm bed and even warmer man with this on his conscience. He waited until they uncuffed Cooper to join him in the office. Once the cops cleared out, he motioned for Cooper to stand. "Let's go."

. . .

Cooper stood, grabbing a dirty duffle bag.

Rocky held up his hand. "No. That has to stay behind."

"Fuck you. You're not stealing my stuff."

Rocky rolled his eyes. "Nobody wants your stuff, but you're not taking that dirty—likely lice-infested—shit in the house."

Cooper's light green eyes flashed with anger. "My shit isn't lice-infested."

"I can call the cops back."

Cooper eyed the bag and then Rocky. Finally, he stepped over the bag and followed Rocky outside. Rocky waited for him. They walked side by side to the house. "Are you an addict?"

. . .

"Fuck you. I ain't no junkie."

Rocky sighed. "Do you have any other retorts?"

Cooper didn't respond.

Rocky took the silence as an opening to ask more questions. "Have you ever held a job?"

"Nobody's gonna hire someone like me."

"I was thinking about it if you could drop the attitude for half a goddamn minute."

Cooper snorted. "This isn't your house. Your pants cost forty dollars at best."

. . .

Rocky couldn't argue. "No. It's not my house, but this is my security team and I'm free to hire anyone I want. The pay is good, and you'd have a roof over your head and food in your stomach, as long as you do your job and everything you can to protect the people living here." Rocky would never take this risk if Zayn and Spencer were in town. Luckily, they had taken a year to tour the world. There were three months left in their trip. If the kid didn't work out, Rocky would replace whatever he stole. Rocky risked his whole ass on this. He bet a lot on Cooper being loyal for a home.

"I'd be living here? What would I have to do, for real? No one offers something like this for nothing."

Rocky got it. He had felt the same when Zayn had made the same offer to him all those years ago. At the time, Rocky would have done anything. If Zayn had been taking him in to be his personal dick sucker, Rocky would have signed on the dotted line. He had been looking at years in prison if Zayn filed charges against him for auto theft. It was better to be a free and paid whore than an incarcerated one.

. . .

"It's as I said. You'd be a guard. The owner here offered me the same deal when I was a few years older than you and I stole his car."

Cooper looked his way. "No way you stole anyone's car."

A chuckle burst from Rocky at Cooper's surprise. "I definitely did, and it was the only time I got caught. It was the dumbest luck ever that I got busted by Zayn. That dumb luck has passed to you. I'm hoping you're as smart as I was and take the deal. It's easy work, unless you have to tackle a trespasser. Otherwise, it's pretty boring, but you'd have an amazing life."

Cooper looked around. Rocky could tell he was trying not look excited, but Rocky felt the hope rolling off him. "Does this place get a lot of trespassers?"

. . .

Rocky nodded. "Mostly press, trying to get a picture of Zayn and Spencer." Rocky led Cooper through a service entrance so he wouldn't immediately spot Zayn's overabundance of wealth.

Cooper eyed everything as they passed. "Who are Zayn and Spencer?"

"The owners."

Cooper shoved his hands in his pockets, as if afraid to touch anything. "Why does everyone want their pictures?"

Rocky led Cooper into the closest furnished bedroom. If Cooper planned to run the moment Rocky left him alone, he didn't want the guy running past a hundred things to steal on the way out. "I'll tell you all about them when you start work in the morning. For now, you can have this room. Hang out here for a few minutes, and I'll grab you some bed linens and whatnot."

.   .   .

Cooper nodded. He still looked distrustful, but the attitude was gone. Rocky prayed he wasn't making the biggest mistake of his life. He needed help.

———————

It was just like Rocky to take in a homeless kid. Jinx would do anything he could to help. Still, he was a bit nervous as he helped Rocky carry everything Cooper would need to start a new life. Jinx had landed two sexy men by sheer luck because people rarely liked him. It was totally Jinx's fault. Jinx was an introvert. He didn't make friends easily.

That was why he followed Rocky into the room, staying hidden behind Rocky's huge body. "Hey, you're still here."

Rocky sounded way too surprised for Jinx's comfort.

.   .   .

"Yeah, well. I need a job and I have to start somewhere."

Jinx peeked around Rocky's large frame. Cooper was about the same size as Jinx and had beautiful light green eyes. "Hey, Cooper."

Cooper looked ready to bolt until Rocky stepped aside. Then Cooper's gaze dropped to Jinx's toes, and he eyed Jinx in a very un-hostile way. "Hey."

"This is my man, Jinx," Rocky said, introducing him. "He's about your size and has some clothes you can have."

Cooper looked between them several times. "Your man. Like dating?"

Jinx found himself taking a half a step behind Rocky to block Cooper. Sometimes, the most violent hate could come from the most unexpected places.

. . .

Rocky didn't seem bothered. "Yeah, like dating. Be nice."

Cooper looked between them again several times. He visibly swallowed. "My mom put me out two years ago for being gay. I guess it's a lot easier for someone as big as you."

Jinx pressed his hand to his chest. This kid's mom had put him out into the cold. What kind of person did that? Jinx tried not to show his anger.

"You'll be happy here. No one will judge you."

Cooper smiled.

"Holy shit. He can smile," Rocky said with a laugh.

. . .

Cooper ignored him. "Do you live here too, Jinx?"

Jinx nodded. "For now." Jinx could feel Rocky staring a hole into the side of Jinx's face. It was hard to keep from looking Rocky's way. "There are a lot of good people living here. You don't have to worry. We'll let you take a shower or whatever. When you're clean, there's a staff kitchen down the hall on the right. The fridge is fully stocked. Maybe tomorrow, after your first day on the job, I could take you shopping for clothes or whatever."

Cooper shifted from foot to foot, looking uncomfortable. "I don't have any money."

Jinx shrugged. "That's fine. I can spot you for a new wardrobe."

For a moment, Cooper didn't respond. When he did, he sounded tired. "So when does the other shoe drop?"

. . .

In truth, Jinx didn't know how to answer that. He imagined this sudden change in circumstances felt like a trick to someone like Cooper. Jinx took a breath and answered in a different way. "My mom died almost two years ago. Even though I had my own place and didn't need the help financially, Zayn took me in because I needed the help emotionally. I know it's hard to believe, but there are good people left in the world. You just found them."

"You still have to work," Rocky said, obviously intent on being a hard-ass.

Cooper nodded. "I will. This still doesn't feel real, but yeah. I'll do whatever."

Jinx took Rocky's hand. Cooper looked ready to drop. They needed to let him sleep. "We'll let you settle in. You're safe here. We'll see each other tomorrow."

. . .

Rocky let Jinx pull him from the room, but he kept looking over his shoulder. "I'll come by at nine tomorrow morning to get you set up at work, okay?"

"Okay." Cooper followed them to the door and closed it behind them.

Jinx heard the lock turn. No doubt the poor kid thought he would be molested or dragged into the street. It wouldn't happen. Jinx invaded Rocky's space. "Softy."

Rocky looked away, but Jinx saw the way his cheeks turned pink. "Yeah, well."

Jinx laughed as he pressed his lips to Rocky's chest. "You're such a teddy bear. I love you."

Rocky snatched Jinx from his feet and tossed him over his shoulder, tearing a loud squeal from Jinx. Jinx covered his mouth, trying to stifle his laughter.

Rocky swatted his ass. "Teddy bear. I'll show you a bear. Don't think I've forgotten that I still owe you for earlier." Rocky stormed toward his bedroom. Jinx caught a glimpse of Cooper peeking out his door at them while Jinx tried pushing his way off Rocky's shoulder without luck. Giving up, Jinx relaxed into his fate. It wasn't like he didn't want to get punished. He couldn't think about anything else. It would be a long night. Jinx couldn't wait.

SEVEN

BETWEEN GETTING Cooper settled and Jinx acting suspicious, the days flew. Wednesday came before Rocky knew it. Then the day screeched to a halt. By the time Rocky headed to Hudson's—alone because Jinx weirdly wasn't home—Rocky was ready to crawl out of his skin if it got him to Hudson faster. When the black and gold gate to Hudson's property came into view, a smile exploded across Rocky's face. He had to stop himself from bouncing in his seat.

After punching in the code, the gate opened, and an unexpected laugh burst from Rocky—like his body couldn't contain his happiness any longer. It had been way too long since Rocky had seen Hudson's gorgeous face in person. Video calls weren't enough. He wanted that warmth he felt when Hudson was in his arms. Rocky needed the scent of Hudson's expensive cologne washing over him. He swore he could already smell Hudson.

Rocky followed the pebble driveway to the front of the house. Rocky parked inside the circle and jumped from his truck. As he jogged up the brick and concrete front steps, the front door opened. Rocky froze. His breath caught at the first sight of Hudson. Until Rocky set eyes on Hudson, he hadn't realized how much he had missed the guy.

Hudson danced in place in his excitement. "You're here."

Rocky ran the last few feet. His mouth covered Hudson's before he managed a word. He fought the urge to shout at the top of his lungs in his happiness. Rocky couldn't stop running his hands over

Hudson's body, as if his mind needed proof Hudson was really there. Hudson tried climbing Rocky like a tree until Rocky grabbed two handfuls of ass and lifted Hudson off his feet. Hudson held on while their kiss went from wild to sweet.

Rocky spoke between kisses. "I'm sorry Jinx isn't with me. He'll be here later."

Hudson dropped his feet to the floor but didn't back away. He buried his face in the crook of Rocky's neck and held on. "I know. He's with Tito. They'll be here any minute."

Confusion had Rocky taking a step back. "Why is Jinx with Tito?"

Hudson twisted his fingers. His gaze moved from side to side, obviously searching for any place to look other than meeting Rocky's stare. "Um... come see what I had done to the bedroom while I was gone." Hudson walked away.

. . .

Rocky followed since Hudson left him no other choice. "What's going on?" He knew something was up. Rocky felt it in his gut.

A loud and fake-sounding laugh trailed down the hall as Hudson quickly marched ahead of him. "Nothing is going on. Well, that's not true. I'm showing you my new bedroom. You have to see it since we'll be sleeping in it soon." He raced around the corner, picking up speed and forcing Rocky to practically jog to keep up. He spoke a mile a minute as he went. "I guess I should wait until Jinx gets here because I don't want to ruin the surprise, but he'll be here soon enough." He led Rocky into his bedroom. "Look. It's a bed big enough for three."

Rocky tore his gaze away from Hudson to stare at the bed. It was big enough for a family of eight, which might have been impressive if Rocky wasn't so damn disturbed by Hudson's behavior. "That's massive. We might lose each other in the middle of the night."

. . .

Hudson went back to twisting his fingers. "I hadn't thought of that. My thought was of comfort. As much as I know we all love cuddling, realistically, we'll have nights when sleep matters when it comes to sleeping in the same bed forever." Hudson's body jerked slightly, as if startled himself. "Fuck. I didn't mean to say that."

Rocky made a dismissive gesture. Hudson was acting off and Rocky needed to know why. "You may as well tell me what's going on. I'm not an idiot. There's obviously something you're keeping from me."

Hudson's shoulders fell. "Okay, but just hear me out, okay?"

"Okay." Even Rocky heard the skepticism in his voice. Thankfully, it didn't stop Hudson's confession.

"Tito is with Jinx because they've been moving Jinx's things out of storage and into some empty rooms around the house all day. They're grabbing the last load of Jinx's things from Zayn's now."

Rocky's heart dropped while his temper hit the ceiling. "What? You two planned for Jinx to move here behind my back?"

Hudson made a calming gesture. "You said you'd hear me out, so listen. He's moving in as a lure to get you here too. I want you both under my roof and in my bed every night. You said you don't want to get married, so live with us instead. Let's be together full time. I want us to be fully committed and under one another's feet. I love you. Let's make this permanent."

A hollow pit opened in Rocky's gut. Jinx had left him to come here, and he didn't understand why no one had talked to him first. "Why didn't you say something? If you had talked to me, we could've saved Jinx a move. I can't leave Zayn. We could live together at his place, sleeping together every night like we did before you left on tour. My job is with Zayn. I have to be there under his roof."

Hudson's forehead screwed up in confusion or pain. Rocky couldn't decide which. "Rocky, you don't need to work. I want to take care of you. I'm not giving up my house and everything I've worked for to go live with a friend like a leech."

A door slammed inside Rocky's heart. He swore he heard the echo of his emotions closing inside his head. "A leech? Is that what you think I am?"

Hudson started pacing, making Rocky nervous. He looked a bit off. His erratic behavior seemed to be about more than just the current topic. "I'm sorry. That's not what I meant. Why didn't I wait for Jinx?" Hudson ran a hand through his Mohawk, making it look a spiky mess. "I'm such an idiot. I knew I couldn't do this alone. Jinx is the one you want. He's the one you'll listen to. There's no reason for you to choose me over Zayn. Goddamn it. I knew I would fuck this up."

. . .

The longer Rocky watched Hudson come unglued, the more obvious it became that something wasn't right. He had only seen Hudson this out of touch one time—the night he had tried leaping from the balcony. Rocky tried calming him. "You're not an idiot. Let's just talk it out. We can make a plan."

Hudson shook his head and kept pacing. "No. There's nothing to say. I get it. Obviously, I'm no prize. I have nothing to offer. You're in this for Jinx and I took him away."

"That's not true."

It was like Hudson couldn't hear him—as if he had gone away. A pocketknife appeared in Hudson's hand. He flipped it open and closed while he paced, looking more despondent by the second. "Jinx won't stay once he knows you won't live with me too. I just wanted the three of us to be together. The last six months have been hell. I thought we could finally find some normalcy. People think I'm nuts for being in this relationship. Maybe they're right. It's obvious I'm the unwanted one."

Rocky didn't think Hudson even knew Rocky was there anymore. It was like he had spiraled into some state of mania. He didn't know what to do. Rocky felt helpless. "Just give me some time to figure things out, okay? I'm in charge of Zayn's security team. There's a lot of responsibility at Zayn's that requires a full-time on-site person. If I'm not there, I need to find someone to replace me. That's difficult."

Hudson shook his head. His feet never stopped moving. The knife never stopped clicking. "Don't patronize me. I know I'm fucked up in the head and you just want it to stop. You think I'm crazy and just want to get away. I get it. Just go. Take Jinx and leave. I know that's what you really want anyhow. I'm just in the way. At least fucking marry him, though. If you plan to take everything from me, at least do that. Maybe it's best if I get out of the way. Losing both of you is like a nightmare. I don't know why I can't wake up. This is what I get for letting myself hope. I wanted too much, and life is reminding me I'm not allowed to be happy. People like me never find one person to love them, much less two." In his downward spiral, Hudson pressed the tip of the knife against his palm and spun. Rocky's heart stopped before racing into his throat as he watched a bead of blood pool around the knifepoint. He honestly didn't think Hudson even knew he was bleeding. That was how far he was gone. Rocky couldn't take it. He needed to make this stop.

"Stop it, Hudson. I love you. I want to be with you. Give me time to make it happen. I'm not like Jinx. It's not possible for me to drop everything and move, but I want to be with you."

Hudson stopped pacing, but the madness didn't leave his eyes. "It's okay, Rocky. I know you don't really love me. It's not possible for anyone to love the real me."

. . .

The devastation in Hudson's expression nearly took out Rocky's knees. He didn't understand what was happening with Hudson, but he knew he had to try to save him. Without thinking things through, Rocky dropped to one knee. "Marry me. If that's what it takes to make you understand I love you every bit as much as I love Jinx, then this is what I'll do. I would gladly be your husband if you'll stop and see how much I love you and want to be here."

"Oh."

Rocky's head whipped around at the sound of surprise coming from the open doorway.

Jinx stood there, looking between them and taking in the scene. It didn't take long for Jinx to correctly surmise the situation. He looked devastated as he motioned between them. "I see." He visibly swallowed. "I guess I'll get out of the way, then."

. . .

Rocky jumped to his feet. "No. That's not..." He rubbed his forehead. There was no way to explain without admitting he was trying to save Hudson from melting down. That might drive Hudson completely over the edge. He was in the worst position he had ever been in, and that said a lot. He had no fucking clue what had happened to his life in the last fifteen minutes. "I just..." Rocky made a helpless gesture.

Jinx nodded. "I see."

"You don't." Rocky knew he didn't because he looked leveled and done.

Jinx nodded again. It was a jerky motion. He walked away. Rocky and Hudson chased after him.

Hudson called out, trying to stop him. "Where are you going, baby? I just got home."

. . .

Jinx didn't slow or look their way. "You're right. You should get to relax and enjoy your marriage proposal." Jinx snatched up his keys from the tray by the door. He didn't even slow to put on his shoes before he was out the door. Tito quickly stepped aside to keep from getting run over. He looked stoic with a box still in his arms. Hudson followed Jinx out, begging for Jinx to stay and talk about this.

Rocky's feet seemed to stick to the living room floor. He couldn't budge. Everything beautiful about his life fell apart around him and he was helpless. All Rocky wanted was to make Hudson well. Hudson was obviously at the edge of another breakdown and doubting their relationship and anyone's ability to love him. Rocky hadn't meant to hurt Jinx. He hadn't been thinking.

Hudson stormed back into the house. His face was red, and his features were hard. He pointed the still open pocketknife at Rocky. "What in the fuck did you just do? You knew he wanted to get married. You swore you never wanted that. How could you do that to him? To us?"

. . .

Rocky made a helpless gesture. Everything was slipping through his fingers. "I just didn't want you to doubt us anymore. You're always gone and I—"

"So this is somehow my fault? No. Just no. You're right. I'm always gone, and it hurts me. My heart is always here with you two and it's hard. I've never had the greatest mental health, but you knew that going in. What would've happened if I said yes? You just pushed him out—like he didn't even matter. That was never supposed to happen."

Rocky couldn't think straight. Everything hurt. "You told me to marry Jinx. Now you're against marriage? Now I'm destroying us?"

Hudson tugged at his own hair, as if the frustration of everything was too much. "Don't you get it? I'm okay with being the outsider. Being with Jinx and you is all I need. I don't need a piece of paper to tell me this is forever. All I wanted tonight was to feel all the love I've been denied the last six months. That's it, and you drove part of us away. How could you shit on us like that?"

Rocky felt completely powerless. Words failed him. One second, they had been on the verge of a great night. The next, they were here. As he looked on, Hudson found his phone and had it to his ear. Jinx's phone rang on the coffee table. A roar tore from Hudson. He threw his phone so hard, it left a hole in the wall before crashing to the floor. His crazed gaze landed on Rocky. "I want you out."

Rocky opened his mouth. No words came out.

Hudson shook his head. "I don't want to hear anything you have to say. I just want you gone."

Before Rocky could find his voice, Tito took his arm and dragged him toward the door. Rocky's gaze stayed glued on Hudson. Hudson went back to pacing and tugging his hair. Rocky's throat swelled to nearly closed. Outside, Tito forced Rocky to look at him. He snapped his fingers in Rocky's face until he had his full attention.

"Listen. You can't help him right now. He's in the middle of an episode. There's nothing you can do. Being here is only making things worse. Let him get back on his meds and calm down. You can't fix anything until then."

Rage and hurt had Rocky lashing out at Tito. "What in the fuck are you taking about?"

Tito's expression snapped closed. "You really don't know, do you?"

Rocky was on the verge of throwing hands just to let some pain loose. "Know what?"

. . .

"Hudson is bipolar. He's having a manic episode."

Rocky's gaze shot to the door. He wanted to rush back inside.

As if reading his mind, Tito kept a tight grip on Rocky's arm to keep him from going anywhere. "You can't help him. He's upset, and until he figures out what over-the-top thing he needs to do to bring himself back down, there's no way for you to force it. He's off his meds. You cannot fix him. I need you to go."

"I can't go," Rocky said, practically screaming in Tito's face. "He needs me."

"Jinx needs you," Tito said, sounding completely calm. His steady voice brought Rocky back to reality. Jinx was out there somewhere, hurting and thinking Rocky planned to push him out. Tito was the best person to help Hudson. Rocky could work on fixing things with Jinx. Then the three of them could talk once Hudson pulled through.

"Okay. You're right. Go help Hudson. I'll find Jinx."

Tito looked relieved, which didn't make Rocky feel better. It only proved Tito was more worried about Hudson than he let on. Rocky watched Tito jog back inside. His eyes stung as reality came bursting through his walls like the Kool-Aid man. He bent at the waist and braced his hands on his knees, trying to catch his breath. Rocky didn't understand what had happened. He had raced over here to have an amazing night with the men he loved. Now everything was gone. It didn't make sense. All he knew was he had lost everything, and he was fairly certain it was all his fault.

The Back Porch was an everyone-knows-your-name coffeehouse. Jinx hadn't been there in a long time. Since moving in with Zayn, the place wasn't as convenient, and Jinx had been busy. Now he didn't know where else to go. He couldn't go home. Hell, technically, Jinx didn't have a home any longer. When Zayn had asked Jinx to come live with him, Jinx had given up his apartment. Between his mom's life insurance money and not having any bills for nearly two years, Jinx had a hefty savings, but still. He didn't know where to go.

Until a few hours ago, most of Jinx's things had been in storage. Now they were scattered throughout Hudson's home. All Jinx had now were the things that had been at Zayn's. Those were in the AMG Zayn had given him for his birthday. That sat in the parking lot of the coffeehouse. Jinx supposed that meant he could go anywhere. After all, he had lived without his stuff in storage for a long time. What did it matter if they belonged to Hudson now? Hudson and Rocky could enjoy Jinx's old furnishings in their new life together... without Jinx.

Jinx wrapped his fingers around his steaming cup and tried breathing through the pain. A tear slipped down his cheek. Jinx quickly wiped it away before anyone saw. He worried if anyone showed him an ounce of compassion, he would fall apart. Jinx couldn't understand how he had been so blind. Everything made sense now. Rocky hadn't made a move on Jinx until he could make a move on Hudson too. After all, Jinx and Rocky had lived under the same roof for months before he confessed to wanting to be with Jinx and Hudson. Jinx wondered how long they had been planning this. He wondered when they had planned to break the news to him. It would have been nice if one of them had said something before Jinx moved half his stuff to Hudson's place. Now Jinx had nowhere to go.

Jinx had a lot of questions. He would never get the answers, and that was for the best. Sometimes he could be pretty weak. That was probably why they had gotten tired of him and made a plan to push him out. Damn. He had been a huge fool. Hudson had talked Jinx out of Zayn's house. All Rocky had to do was give him the final push from Hudson's life. Boom. A new relationship without Jinx all tied up in a pretty bow. No ugliness of getting Jinx out of Zayn's place after the breakup. He hadn't known people could be so cruel.

. . .

"Are you okay?"

Jinx quickly averted his eyes as Wrecker, the shop's owner, came to stand over him. He nodded while fighting the urge to swipe at his eyes. "I'm just plotting my next move in life."

Wrecker sat without invitation. It wasn't like Jinx could complain. Wrecker owned the place. Jinx's gaze slid the man's way. He had gorgeous dark skin and beautiful eyes. They were like a lion's. Mesmerizing. Jinx had heard the guy used to be a professional football player before opening this coffeehouse. He could see it. Wrecker looked like he could wreck someone.

"Do you need someone to talk to?"

A humorless bark of laughter burst from Jinx. "I wouldn't even know where to start."

· · ·

Wrecker nodded, looking understanding. "Without thinking too hard about it, say the first thing that would make things better right now in this moment."

Since Jinx had nothing left to lose, he said the first thing that popped into his mind. "I need a new life in a new place with a fresh start." Some place he wouldn't have to watch the loves of his life marry without him, Jinx silently added.

Wrecker sat back and eyed Jinx for a moment before glancing around the room. His gaze landed on a couple in the corner. One guy was skinny and perfectly styled, wearing a suit that made him look like a pimp. His date had long blond hair and a body that would make any gay man weep. Wrecker tapped his knuckles on the table. "Give me a second. I might have exactly what you need."

Jinx watched Wrecker cross the room and chat with the gorgeous couple. Their gazes turned Jinx's way, and Jinx found himself staring at his coffee. He hated everyone knowing he was falling apart.

. . .

After a few minutes of chatting, Wrecker returned. He sat across from Jinx. "Those are my friends, Brett and Roman. Roman moved here from Colorado after he fell in love with Brett, but he still owns a home there. If you really want to..." Wrecker's gaze slid past Jinx's shoulder. He visibly tried grasping the threads of their conversation. "If you'd really like to start over..."

A familiar gigantic bald bodyguard blocked their table from onlookers as the chair beside Jinx suddenly became occupied. "There you are. Would you please listen to me?"

Jinx swiped his hand across his eyes. "There's nothing to say, Hudson. Please leave me alone."

"I have a lot to say," Hudson shot back, obviously not intending to leave.

. . .

"The man asked you to leave him alone."

At Wrecker's hard tone, Tito ruffled. "Stay the fuck out of this."

Wrecker stood, going nose to nose with the Italian bodyguard—like Tito wasn't inhuman in size. "This is my coffeehouse. I say who stays and who goes."

Jinx wished the floor would open and swallow him whole, but this was his mess. "It's okay, Wrecker. I've got it."

Wrecker's gaze slid his way. His features didn't soften. "If you're sure, I have customers." He stared hard at Tito. "But if you need me, just shout. I'm not scared to put a man down."

Jinx's embarrassment doubled. "Thank you."

. . .

Once Wrecker walked away, Hudson slung his arm across the back of Jinx's chair. "That's better. We need to talk, or rather, I do, so listen. I didn't expect Rocky to do what he did, but it changes nothing. You told me you would marry me, and I bought a ring and everything. So why did you leave me? You're supposed to be with me."

Jinx blinked. Hudson was too animated. His every word came out twice as fast as necessary. Jinx had to fight to keep up. He tried. "Look, I lived with Rocky for months before you two met and he never made a move on me. You didn't want a relationship with me until you got to know Rocky. It's obvious that I'm just in the way of you two wanting each other. I'm out of the way now. Go be with the man you really want." The words ripped and tore at Jinx's throat, slowly killing him. But Jinx loved Hudson and Rocky enough to get out of the way. Loving them was currently killing him.

Hudson shot to his feet and climbed on top of the table. Tito did an amazing job of keeping people away while looking like this was an everyday occurrence. Jinx grabbed Hudson's ankles, scared he would fall.

"What are you doing?"

Hudson dug a ring from his pocket and held it out. "You're supposed to marry me."

Jinx worked hard to keep his jaw from hitting the floor. The ring was fucking amazing and Hudson was yelling at the top of his lungs.

"Get off Wrecker's table and we'll talk about it."

Hudson shook his head. "Not until you say you'll marry me." Hudson glanced around. He pointed at Jinx and yelled at the other customers. "This is the man I want. This one. He said he would marry me when I retired. I'm retiring and now he's trying to take it back." Hudson did a little dance move as he met Jinx's stare again. "I'm not coming down until you agree."

He was ridiculous, and it scared Jinx. Jinx rubbed Hudson's legs. "Please come down before you fall, and I end up on the news as the guy who ruined Hudson Vincent's career."

"I have no career. I told you, I'm retiring. So now it's time to uphold your end of the deal."

Jinx ran his thumbs up Hudson's shins. "Baby, you're going to crash really hard soon. When was the last time you had your meds?"

Hudson didn't budge. "Say you'll marry me, and you can take me home."

Jinx looked Tito's way. "When did he stop his meds?" Jinx tried to keep their conversation as private as possible.

. . .

"Halfway through the tour. He claims they interfere with his performance."

Hudson bounced on the table, pulling Jinx's attention back his way. "You still haven't answered my question."

Jinx's chest hurt. He loved Hudson. Likely he always would. Even though Hudson was obviously having one of his over-the-top manic episodes, he wasn't out of his head. He was just at the crest right before the fall. Jinx had been too hurt to notice earlier. Likely, by tomorrow, Hudson would be crippled by depression or not. Hudson didn't always crash, but he might. Jinx had to get him back on his meds. "If I say yes, will you go home and take your medication?"

"If you go with me."

. . .

Jinx nodded. He loved Hudson too much to let this go on. "Then yes. I'll marry you."

Hudson let out a loud shout and leaped from the table. Thankfully, Tito obviously anticipated Hudson's jump and kept him from getting hurt. Several people clapped when Hudson slipped the ring on Jinx's finger before kissing him. Jinx's heart melted as their lips met. He fought the urge to cry again. The night had been awful and heartbreaking. He didn't know how to feel. Jinx wanted to marry Hudson. He wasn't scared of Hudson's issues, but things were still a mess. It was supposed to be the three of them. They were supposed to be convincing Rocky to live with them. Jinx didn't know if Hudson's marriage proposal was real or part of his uncontrolled disorder. Nothing felt right, but he believed in love. Right now, Hudson needed Jinx. Tomorrow, he would likely need Jinx even more. Jinx would have to figure out the future later. He didn't belong to himself. Jinx had always belonged to Hudson. It was time to go to his new home.

The mind was a terrifying thing. Hudson's most especially. It was a prison with no windows or bars. Sometimes, his brain and mood turned against him, making everything a horrible nightmare he couldn't escape. Despite that, he wasn't crazy or dumb. He also wasn't blind or deaf. Hudson saw and heard everything he did and said. He just couldn't stop. After Rocky had left, Hudson's mind had fixated on marrying Jinx. He had convinced himself that if he could achieve that, then he had found the holy grail of happiness. If he could marry Jinx, then maybe he wasn't a complete piece of shit.

Jinx was amazing, though. He took Hudson back home, and together they carried the last of Jinx's things inside. With Tito's help, it hadn't taken long to get Jinx completely moved in. Jinx had given up a lot when he had gone to live with Zayn. He had sacrificed even more to be with Hudson, but at least he would have all his things in one place. Hudson was more than aware he was a complete mess. He wasn't hallucinating this time around. At least, Hudson didn't think so. He took his meds while standing at the kitchen counter and with Jinx watching. Jinx was right. Hudson would likely crash soon. He wanted to make love to Jinx before it happened. Maybe then Jinx wouldn't leave.

"I'm sorry."

A sweet smile touched Jinx's face. "Please stop apologizing."

A wave of sadness washed over Hudson. He had a hard time keeping it at bay. "No. I embarrassed you. That's not the proposal I planned. You deserve so much better than what happened tonight. I don't even understand. We were supposed to be starting a new chapter tonight. I'm so fucking sorry." Hudson's voice broke. He was such a fuck-up.

Jinx crowded his space. "Tell me what you planned for your proposal." His smile was hard to resist. Hudson clung to that while trying to breathe through the pain. "Um, I rented out that French restaurant you like. The place with the three-month wait for reservations."

. . .

"Really?" Jinx sounded and looked happy.

That kept Hudson talking. "Yeah. I planned to watch you order all your favorite things. Then, at dessert, the server was supposed to bring out a tablet with a video to show off all our highlights together."

Jinx held Hudson tighter and laughed. "Please tell me the clip of you telling everyone to suck your dick on the Tyler show was in the video."

"Definitely."

Jinx laughed harder, and some of the darkness retreated. Hudson tried harder to stay afloat. "Then once I had you all teary-eyed, I planned to drop to one knee."

. . .

"That's a good plan. Romantic. Well thought out. I don't know, though. It doesn't quite have the flair of standing on a table in the middle of a coffeehouse."

Hudson couldn't resist any longer. He kissed the corner of Jinx's mouth. "I'd do anything to keep you. I don't care what people think. Only you."

"And Rocky," Jinx said, holding Hudson's stare.

A shot of pain tried taking out his knees. "I can't talk about that yet."

Jinx nodded and rubbed Hudson's chest, as if trying to calm him. "Okay. Tell me how I can make your first night back home perfect."

Hudson didn't have to think about it. "Go to bed with me. Let me make love to my fiancé."

. . .

Jinx's expression turned wicked. "There's nothing I want more. Let me talk to Tito really quick. I need to ask him to grab something for me I forgot, but then I'll be ready for bed. Is that okay?"

Hudson let go of Jinx's waist. "Of course. Just hurry. I've spent the last six months miserable."

Jinx pressed a quick kiss to Hudson's lips and pulled away. "I'll be back before you can miss me."

He really was. Jinx jogged from the kitchen, was gone half a minute, and was back. Hunger hit Hudson like a ton of bricks at the sight of Jinx walking toward him. "I love you." Even to his ears, the claim sounded harsh.

A sweet smile touched Jinx's lips. "I love you too."

· · ·

"Please tell me you forgive me for ruining everything." Tears pressed at the backs of Hudson's eyes. The crash was coming faster than expected.

Jinx's body collided with his. "Stop thinking."

Hudson didn't have much choice. His tongue was in Jinx's mouth and Jinx's hand was inside Hudson's pants before he knew it would happen. Heat exploded through him. Hudson tore at Jinx's clothes. His madness changed directions. He needed to please Jinx. Hudson wanted to hear Jinx cry his name. If he could blow Jinx's mind, maybe Jinx could forgive him for destroying everything. Jinx didn't protest when his bare ass hit the cold marble island. Hudson didn't give him time to think about it. He leaned over and swallowed Jinx's cock. Jinx held his hair while Hudson licked and sucked. He was consumed with a need to make Jinx scream. Saliva ran down his hands while Hudson went wild on Jinx's cock. He used the mess to finger and stretch Jinx's asshole. Moans caressed his ear. They fed his madness. He needed things to move faster. His brain sped at a thousand miles an hour. Hudson wanted everything else to keep up.

In a flash, he shot upward and towed Jinx from the island. Jinx scrambled to hang on to the edge so he wouldn't fall on the floor as Hudson impaled him. The instant Jinx's hot hole engulfed his dick, Hudson froze. His heart raced. His anxiety hit a wall. He started hyperventilating.

"I forgot the condom."

His chest caved. Each breath came harder than the last. Jinx would never forgive him now. Everything he did was wrong. He was worthless. Hudson didn't know why Jinx bothered with him. Everyone would be better off if he died. Then they would be free of his abject stupidity.

Jinx stroked his face. "Shhh. It's okay. Breathe. We're getting married. It's okay."

· · ·

Air filled his lungs. His mind cleared. His heart slowed. Hudson took another breath. It sounded strained—like a drowning man—but his mind got even clearer. They were getting married. This was a commitment. Hudson hadn't slept with anyone other than Jinx and Rocky since they started dating. That meant he hadn't slept with anyone else since the last time he got tested. He also never had unprotected sex with anyone. Hudson took another breath. He wasn't endangering Jinx. They were making love. This was a benefit of knowing there would be no one else. It was just them now.

Hudson rocked forward. A gasp escaped Jinx. He did it again. Jinx felt amazing on Hudson's cock.

"I love you." That was all the warning Hudson gave before he took what he wanted. Hudson pumped and rolled his hips, finding the angle that made Jinx moan. Once he was there, he didn't stop. Hudson pounded, riding the high of Jinx's open pleasure. He stared at Jinx, refusing to blink against the sight of Jinx moving closer to release. When hot cum hit Hudson's chest, he lost it. He took Jinx to the floor. It was hard on his knees, but Hudson didn't care. All his focus was on filling Jinx's ass with cum. He needed to own him. Hudson pounded while focused on one goal: orgasm. His muscles clenched as his balls drew up tight. Everything finally slowed inside his mind. When the first spasm hit, the air left his lungs. Hudson cried Jinx's name as he rode out the waves. As he collapsed, Jinx was there to catch him. When he fell apart, Jinx stayed to put him back together.

EIGHT

THE SHOCK EBBED a hair as Rocky stared at the wall. It had taken a few hours of sitting alone in his private living room, but reality slowly returned. He didn't like it. The truth was ugly. Rocky had fucked up everything. That was no easy feat, but Rocky had figured out how to do it. Oddly, he wasn't surprised about losing Hudson. Hudson had always been a dream. Jinx, though, Rocky hadn't thought he could lose him. It wasn't that Jinx was more in his league than Hudson. He wasn't. But Jinx was more loyal than most people and usually saw beyond Rocky's bullshit. Not tonight. Tonight, Rocky had gone too far. Rocky had searched every place he could think to look without luck. Jinx was nowhere to be found. Finally, he had come home, praying Jinx would be here. He wasn't. He was gone.

Jinx's expression wouldn't leave Rocky's mind. Rocky had leveled him. He had known Jinx wanted to get married someday. Jinx had stayed with Rocky, even though he knew Rocky didn't want to be anyone's husband. Rocky had spit in the face of that sacrifice. The betrayal had been too much. Rocky felt sick. He had hurt someone he was supposed to protect. Rocky didn't know if he could live with that. Then there was Hudson.

Rocky had known there was something wrong with Hudson. Something Rocky's love couldn't fix. But Rocky was an emotional repairman, and he had to try to make everyone happy. He had destroyed Jinx to pull Hudson away from the edge and lost them both in his effort. Rocky didn't know where to go with the pain. Hudson needed him, and Rocky couldn't be there. The helplessness choked him. Jinx was out there somewhere, thinking the worst of Rocky. Hudson believed Rocky would fuck over Jinx to be with him. Rocky wanted to smash everything he owned in a fit of rage. His skin crawled with the need to do something. To fix everything. Rocky didn't know where to start.

"This dude is here to see you."

Rocky startled as Cooper's voice cut through his inner panic. Since Cooper was still jumpy and unsure of his place, Rocky tried tempering his reaction as he looked the kid's way. A gigantic Tito stood at Cooper's back, looking like a finely dressed thug dwarfing the tiny blond.

"Thanks, Cooper."

Cooper smiled like he had been given the highest of praises. "No problem." He cast a quick glance Tito's way before scurrying away. Tito didn't wait for an invitation. He chose a chair and sat.

"Jinx sent me."

. . .

Rocky's spine gave out at just the sound of Jinx's name, leaving him no choice but to lean back in his chair. "Is he okay?"

Tito nodded. "Hudson went after him. He convinced Jinx to come home. Jinx made Hudson take his meds." Tito paused, as if torn over whether he should speak. His loyalty to Hudson couldn't be clearer. Finally, he met Rocky's stare as if determined to power through. "He's bipolar 1, so he might crash after this manic episode or he might not. Nine times out of ten, he's fine after the episodes pass, but this was a big one."

"Thanks to me for stressing him out," Rocky guessed.

Tito flashed him a humorless smile, proving Rocky's thoughts were right. "It's not all you. He stopped taking his meds about three months ago. I've tried talking to him about it, but I'm just an employee."

. . .

Rocky wanted to argue that wasn't true, but he was in the same boat with Zayn. If he worried about anything Zayn did, he could argue and fuss, but in the end, he was just an employee. "I'm glad Jinx got him to take his meds."

Tito nodded. "Me too." He cleared his throat and glanced around the room, as if uncomfortable with having this conversation, but Tito pressed on. "Like I said, Jinx asked me to come by and update you. Hudson is refusing to talk about what happened, so Jinx was afraid to call until after this episode passes. He needs to get Hudson calm, but he understands you didn't know and probably freaked when you saw Hudson in a full-blown attack."

Rocky's throat tried swelling closed. They were still over, nonetheless. "I understand."

"Try not to worry. Hudson has fired me countless times over the years. I just stopped paying attention and refuse to leave. He's usually over it by the time hallucinations end."

. . .

Rocky swiped his hand over his eyes. Everything was so much worse than he had known. Hudson hallucinated. That sounded terrible. His babies were suffering, and Rocky couldn't be there to help. "I don't know what to do." The confession slipped out before Rocky could think better of speaking.

Tito nodded. "I know. It's hard being the strong one. I've been dealing with this for years, but there's a reason I brought Hudson to Jinx the night he tried swan diving from the balcony. Jinx wears his every emotion on his sleeve. That's what drew Hudson to him. Hudson knows Jinx won't judge him for being human."

"And he thinks I will," Rocky supplied, feeling defeated.

Tito shook his head. "It's not that. You're the strong one. He can't talk about what happened today for the same reason he fires me once a month. It makes him feel weak and broken to be seen like this by someone like us. He needs you because you're the strong one, but Jinx needs Hudson even when Hudson can't be strong. Jinx never sees him as weak."

"I don't see him as weak." The words sounded angry even to Rocky's ears. He couldn't help it. The helplessness crippled him and pissed him off. He hated Hudson thought badly of him.

"I know you don't. This will pass. He'll need you when it's over."

Rocky wasn't as sure. It sounded to him like Hudson needed Jinx and Rocky was in the way. Jinx had obviously known Hudson was bipolar. Rocky hadn't. Jinx could keep Hudson doing what he needed to do to stay healthy. Rocky was just some guy who had gotten really, really lucky to hold the sun and stars for a while. Now he needed to move aside so they could flourish without him holding them back.

. . .

Rocky took a steadying breath. "Thanks for keeping me posted. I would have paced the floor all night."

A humorless chuckle rumbled from Tito. "Don't lie. You'll still walk the floor all night."

A smile Rocky didn't feel stretched his lips. "Yeah. I suppose I will." But he would have to get over it, eventually. Hudson and Jinx weren't his anymore. He had to let them go so they could thrive.

Tito stood and patted Rocky's shoulder before leaving him alone. He heard voices rumble in the hall but couldn't make out the words. Rocky wasn't surprised when Cooper slipped silently into the chair Tito had abandoned. Cooper spent most of his nights quietly sitting with Rocky and Jinx—like he was scared they would disappear if he let them out of his sight.

Tonight, Cooper found his voice. "Is Jinx cheating on you?"

. . .

A smile Rocky didn't feel snapped to his lips. It was obvious Cooper had been eavesdropping. "No. It's complicated."

"Oh." Cooper stared at him in silence for a few seconds before digging for more. "Was he cheating on this Hudson guy with you?"

"No. The three of us were together."

Cooper's mouth fell open. "Like together, together, and you knew about it?"

A laugh burst from Rocky. "To be honest, I don't know how to explain it to anyone else. The three of us spent time together and fell in love with one another. We decided we didn't care what people thought, and yeah. We were a throuple."

. . .

Cooper nodded. He looked engrossed. "Where has this Hudson been?"

"On tour."

"You mean he's famous." Cooper nearly screeched the words.

Rocky smiled at Cooper's shock. "Yeah. He's pretty famous."

"Would I know him?"

Rocky shrugged. "I guess that depends on what kind of music you like. It's Hudson Vincent."

Cooper shot forward in his seat. "Are you fucking kidding me? You're dating Hudson fucking Vincent?"

. . .

Rocky's smile fell. "Not anymore."

"Oh." Cooper's excitement visibly drained away. He sat back. "They kicked you out of the band."

A lump formed in Rocky's throat. "I think I kicked myself out of the band by being stupid."

Cooper toyed with the hem of his shirt, twisting it and stretching the material. "What did you do?"

Rocky swallowed down the pain. "I asked Hudson to marry me."

Cooper visibly swallowed. When he spoke, his voice sounded small and hurt. "You wanted to shut out Jinx. Why? He's so nice, and he talks about you like you're the love of his life. I don't understand."

· · ·

Rocky didn't know what to say. He didn't understand either. Hudson had been unreachable. Rocky thought he could save him. Instead, he had hurt everyone. Tito was right. Hudson needed Jinx. Rocky had always been alone. He could go back to that. Hudson wouldn't make it without Jinx. Rocky loved them. That meant getting out of the way. Loving them enough to let them go. Cooper still stared at him, waiting patiently for an answer.

Rocky said the only truth that mattered now. "Like I said, I'm dumb." Rocky looked away. The whys didn't matter now. He had lost everything. There was no going back. Hudson and Jinx were better off without him. That was that.

Jinx: *Hudson is sleeping. You should come back so we can talk.*

Rocky: *I'm glad he's getting some sleep. I don't think that's a good idea.*

· · ·

Jinx: *I'm sorry I lost my temper. Please don't let that be the thing that ruins us.*

Rocky: *You didn't do anything wrong. I did. Please, just be happy. Hudson needs you.*

Jinx: *And I need you.*

Rocky: *No, you don't. You should go cuddle with Hudson. He might not be in his right mind when he wakes up. You should be there for him.*

Jinx: *Who'll be there for you?*

Rocky: *Don't worry about me. Just be happy.*

Jinx: *Please don't make me beg.*

. . .

Rocky: *Don't. Just get some sleep. Hudson needs you and he won't let me be there. I need you to love him enough for the both of us. Give him a life I can't.*

Jinx: *Stop talking like we're over. You're breaking my heart.*

Rocky: *I'm breaking mine too. I love you both. Be happy.*

For longer than he cared to admit, Jinx stared at his phone, silently begging Rocky to text him again. To call. Anything. Mostly, he wanted a sign they weren't over. Nothing happened.

"He won't come back."

Hudson's claim had Jinx scrambling to put his phone away and cuddle with Hudson. "No. He won't come back."

· · ·

On their sides, they stared into each other's eyes. Only the light spilling from the bathroom illuminated the room enough for Jinx to see Hudson's clear gaze. He was doing better, except now there was pain in Hudson's expression. "It's my fault."

Jinx shook his head. "It's not. It's mine. I got my feelings hurt and stormed out. I didn't know you were having an episode. He probably didn't know how to react."

"I should've told him. I just didn't want to look weak in his eyes."

Jinx stroked Hudson's cheek. "Baby, you're not weak. This isn't something you can control. You were born like this and it's not who you are. This disorder is just part of you, and I love every single thing about you, even that. I wouldn't change a damn thing about you."

. . .

"I missed you so much." Hudson whispered the words as if they tore from his throat. "It was harder this time than it's ever been. All I wanted was to come home."

Jinx's chest hurt. He hated that Hudson struggled. "You should've told me. I would've come to you. Spencer has been out of town, so I haven't had to work. I could've toured with you."

A sad smile touched Hudson's lips. He shook his head. "You would've been miserable being stuck in hotels alone, and Rocky would've been brokenhearted. I can handle a lot, but I can't handle knowing you two are unhappy."

"I love you."

Hudson's gaze moved over Jinx's face, as if searching to see if Jinx told the truth. "I love you too. Do you really want to marry me, or did you only agree to calm me down?"

. . .

Jinx's heart ached for too many reasons to count. They had lost Rocky, and it didn't look like he planned to come back. Rocky was right about one thing, though. Hudson needed him. Rocky obviously didn't. Jinx had to find a way to live with that. "I want to marry you."

Hudson rolled away and climbed from the bed. Jinx watched as Hudson padded across the room in the nude. It was a nice show. Jinx pressed his hand to his stomach. He still felt the same now as he had a couple of years ago when Hudson had kissed him for the first time. Hudson was this extremely famous guy with millions of fans all over the world. He could have anyone. For whatever reason, he wanted Jinx, and it had been humbling. Now Jinx knew the real Hudson, and he couldn't imagine living without him.

After a moment of shifting through his still packed bags, Hudson came out with a tattered-looking notebook. He crawled back into bed with Jinx. He kept moving until he straddled Jinx's body. Jinx's hands smoothed up Hudson's thighs—as if they were drawn to Hudson's skin like a magnet. Everything else fell away. It was only the two of them now.

With Jinx massaging Hudson's thighs, Hudson flipped through the thick book. It had loose pages trying to fall out. They were various colors and sizes, proving Hudson had been putting the pages together for a long time. He spoke as he searched through each one. "Earlier, you said I didn't want to be in an exclusive relationship with you until after I met Rocky. That's not true. I used to hire Spencer to DJ my release parties just so I could see you. I was like four parties in and two hundred thousand dollars spent before I worked up the nerve to make a move."

Jinx snorted at the confession. "You're you and I'm me. I doubt you've ever had to work up the nerve to hit on anyone, much less someone like me."

Hudson stopped his hunt long enough to meet Jinx's stare with an incredulous look. "I am a complete mess and we both know it. Stop acting like I'm some prize. We both know I'm not."

Jinx's throat swelled. "You are to me."

A small smile touched Hudson's lips. He went back to his search. "Everything in this notebook is dated, because I'm crazy and I figure I'll die young. Maybe you can make some money off publishing my thoughts when I'm gone."

"Don't."

Hudson froze again at Jinx's harshly spoken whisper. His gaze didn't waver from the pages this time, as if he couldn't make himself meet Jinx's stare. "My head still isn't right, baby, but I'm trying. I'm sorry you fell in love with me." He went back to shuffling through the pages. He found what he was looking for before Jinx found the words to make Hudson understand he shouldn't be sorry. Jinx didn't regret a thing.

. . .

"Here we go." He flashed the notebook Jinx's way so he could see the date. "I wrote this before I met Rocky. Just listen, okay?"

Jinx nodded. "Okay."

Hudson took an audible breath, and read. "Tonight was the third time I saw him. I wanted to ask if Jinx was his real name, and—if so—if he knew the story behind his name. Instead, we talked about ice cream." Jinx smiled at the memory. They had somehow managed to talk about ice cream for hours. "I don't know why I haven't done anything to gauge his interest. Maybe I'm a little scared he likes me too, and I'll taint someone so beautiful. He already has a sadness in his eyes. I'll only make it worse. But it's funny the way I can't stop thinking about him. He gave me his number so we can try out a new ice cream shop in town when I get back from my next tour. I could tell he doesn't think I'll call. He's right. I won't, but I still programmed his number in my phone under the contact name *Someday*. Someday I'll be better, and someday he'll be the first person I call. I don't know why I'm so certain, but I know he's the one. Someday, he'll see it too."

Tears leaked from the corners of Jinx's eyes and rolled back into his hair. He didn't bother wiping them away. Hudson loved him. Jinx wouldn't let him regret it. "My mom named me Jinx because I was born on a Friday the thirteenth at exactly one o'clock or thirteen hundred hours' military time. I was thirteen days early, and she had unexpectedly gone into labor with me after a black cat crossed her path on the way to her doctor's appointment. She was very superstitious, and I was born the ultimate jinx. Oddly, my life has been extremely unlucky. That is, until I met you. You're that one good thing I don't know what I did to deserve, but I'm not letting go. Maybe I'm your someday, but you're my forever."

Hudson's lips parted as if Jinx surprised him. He looked almost puzzled. While Jinx looked on, Hudson tossed the notebook aside and grabbed his phone. "After you agreed to marry me before I left for my tour, I changed your contact name." He unlocked his phone and turned it Jinx's way so he could see his contact name: *My Forever*.

Jinx's gaze shot to Hudson's. It was like Jinx had been shown a sign. They had been meant to meet and fall in love. Jinx swiped at his eyes as more tears slipped out. He didn't understand how he could lose so much and gain so much on the same day. Yet here he was. Sad and happy. At the bottom and the top. No one had prepared him for this. At the end of the day, he loved Hudson too much to be anything other than the man Hudson believed him to be.

"I can't wait to be your husband."

For a moment, Hudson stared down at Jinx with his heart hidden behind a closed expression. When he finally spoke, his voice had a harsh note. "Then you're a fool, but I'm so goddamn happy for it."

If that didn't sum up their entire relationship, then nothing did. Fool or not, he would love Hudson until his dying breath. Jinx didn't know any other way to be. He had to focus on them now, because if he knew nothing else, he knew he couldn't make Rocky come back. Jinx wasn't strong enough to hold on to two men. He didn't know why he had let himself believe he could be. Rocky had been the one holding the three of them together. Now Rocky was done. Jinx had to get back to reality. His life was with Hudson. He wouldn't fail him.

NINE

HUDSON TRIED. He really did. All his calls and texts to Rocky went unanswered. One day, he woke up and accepted they were done. He couldn't pinpoint the exact moment reality set in. It was more of a slow acknowledgment of the truth. He was too much work for Rocky. His episode had been more than Rocky could handle. Hudson understood. He had driven away many people over the years. This one hurt more than the rest, except maybe his parents. That had been a hard loss. It seemed like everyone he loved the most left the easiest, except Jinx. All Jinx wanted was to be loved in return. That was something Hudson wouldn't fail at doing.

. . .

Hudson watched Jinx chew on the side of his nail while looking through brochures. Everything about Jinx turned Hudson on, but Jinx made Hudson's dick a lot harder today with his sexy outfit. His short shorts and ragged tank top might not be anything special. They seemed to fit his body in all the right ways. Hudson couldn't stop eyeing his sexy legs and ass.

Jinx looked up and caught Hudson ogling him. He smacked Hudson with the brochure. "This is serious business. You have to help me decide."

Hudson shook his head. "I absolutely do not have to do that. This one thing is your decision. I don't have anyone other than Tito to invite to a wedding. So, like I said, you need to be the one to choose. Big wedding, small wedding, or eloping are all fine with me. As long as we're married at the end of the ceremony, let's do what you want."

Jinx's shoulders fell. "I mean, I don't really have much of anyone to invite either. Spencer and Zayn are the only ones who matter enough to invite them. All this shit looks stressful." He held up a brochure. "Chapels." He held up a catalog. "Invitations and tablecloths." Jinx let the stack of papers fall to the floor. "There's so much shit to plan."

A laugh vibrated in Hudson's throat. "You called planning a wedding shit twice in one rant. I have a feeling we should elope."

"Thank you," Jinx said, sounding like a weight lifted from his chest. "I didn't want to be the one to say it, but I agree. Let's just go to Vegas or Aspen or wherever people go to get married. That way, we don't have to plan or wait or make nice with people who don't give a shit about us anyhow."

Hudson couldn't stop smiling. There was nothing he wanted more than to call Jinx his husband. He wanted to be settled into their new life and titles. That way, if he ever lost his battle against his mind, Jinx would get everything Hudson owned. Hudson wanted him to be set.

. . .

"With that settled, where do you want to honeymoon?"

With a loud groan, Jinx threw himself backwards across the couch in full dramatics. Hudson laughed as he stole his chance to pounce. He swapped between tickling Jinx and kissing him. Laughter filled the room, giving Hudson hope and light where there used to be none.

"Hey, Jinx. Cooper is here to see you."

Hudson scrambled away and helped Jinx sit up before looking Tito's way. "I finally get to meet the infamous Cooper." Jinx had told Hudson all about the teen and his antics.

A blond head poked around Tito's body, making Hudson realize the tiny teen was hidden by Tito's large frame.

. . .

"Hi. Holy shit. It really is Hudson Vincent."

Hudson tried not to laugh. Cooper's reaction was a familiar one, but Hudson wasn't used to hearing it inside his home.

"Yay. It's Cooper," Jinx said, bounding to his feet. He crossed the room and pulled Cooper from his hiding spot. They were close to the same size, except Cooper looked malnourished. Jinx hugged him before dragging him across the room to sit with them. Hudson noticed Tito didn't leave them alone. He found it odd that Tito felt he needed to stay to protect Hudson from Jinx's friend.

"You left me," Cooper said the moment he was settled.

Jinx's shoulders fell. "I'm so sorry. Things got kind of complicated, and you got lost in the shuffle, but I'm still around. I promise. How are you settling in at Zayn's?"

"It's okay." Cooper twisted the hem of his shirt, stretching out an already loose-fitting article of clothing. "I think I'm pretty useless as far as security goes. It's a job and a place to live. I can't complain, but I'm super aware it's a pity position. There's no way I'm scaring away anyone sneaking onto the property."

Hudson couldn't take it. He knew what it was like to feel inadequate. "You could always come live here instead. Obviously, I don't have Zayn's money, but we would take care of you."

Cooper flashed Hudson a shy smile. "Thanks for the offer, but I couldn't leave Rocky behind. He took me in and he's already all alone. I can't abandon him."

. . .

Hudson fought hard to keep breathing. "I understand." He was glad Rocky wasn't alone. "We wouldn't want Rocky abandoned either."

Jinx nodded. A pained expression crossed his features. "How is Rocky?"

"Sad," Cooper said, stabbing Hudson in the heart. "He tries to act like nothing is wrong, but he snaps at everyone all day. Then he sits in the silence when he isn't working. I usually sit with him so he isn't alone, but he doesn't really talk to me. He doesn't really talk to anyone." Cooper's gaze moved to the mess of catalogs and brochures on the floor. "I saw a few headlines saying you two are getting married. Nobody has said when, though."

"I'll let you two catch up," Hudson said, pushing to his feet. He needed a moment alone.

Jinx glanced his way, looking worried. "Are you okay?"

. . .

Hudson winked. "Of course. Just yell through the intercom if you need me. I'll be around."

For a moment, Jinx eyed him as if he saw through Hudson's smile. He was never any good at hiding his mood swings from Jinx. Still, Jinx nodded and let him have his moment of peace. After giving Jinx a quick kiss, Hudson wandered aimlessly down the hall. He couldn't listen to any more talk of Rocky. Hudson had tried explaining and apologizing. He had offered so many peace offerings, Hudson didn't know where to start. No matter what he did or said, Rocky wouldn't talk to him. There was no going back, and Hudson would never forgive himself for it. All he could do now was focus on Jinx.

"I saw Jinx and Hudson today."

. . .

At the sound of words Rocky wasn't ready to face, his entire body tensed. He didn't respond. Cooper didn't seem to need Rocky to have a conversation.

"Hudson wasn't anything like I expected. He's so famous. I never expected him to be so nice. He offered to let me come live with them, since I'm no good at pretending to be a security guard."

"You're a perfectly fine security guard, but yeah. Hudson is amazingly human for a superstar."

Cooper nodded as he moved a chess piece. "I was a little disappointed he didn't have the green Mohawk. I always thought that was badass."

"Is he back to pink?" Rocky hated himself for asking.

"Nah. He's shaved his head completely. His hair is growing in brown. I wasn't expecting a normal guy."

· · ·

A sad smile touched Rocky's lips. He fought the urge to rub his chest. Hudson and Jinx felt so far away. It sounded like Hudson was doing well. That was all Rocky could hope for.

"I'm surprised you haven't asked about Jinx, or if I accepted the offer to live with them."

Rocky blew out a breath and tore his gaze away from the chessboard. "Okay. I'll bite. Did you accept their offer?"

Cooper didn't answer right away. His light green eyes seemed to see right through Rocky's bullshit. He had an amazingly old soul beneath his hard veneer. "No. I told them I couldn't leave you alone."

Rocky went back to staring at the board. He wasn't very good at the game, but Cooper was trying to teach him. It took a lot of concentration. Some nights, the distraction was all that saved him. "I'm used to being alone."

. . .

Rocky moved a piece.

Cooper immediately captured it. "That's exactly why I can't leave you. If someone doesn't teach you to tolerate the company of others, you'll never go back to where you belong. Jinx looked amazing, by the way. Damn sexy, actually. He had on these short shorts and a sexy tank top."

"Don't be disrespectful."

Cooper laughed. "So you can get jealous."

Rocky snorted. Cooper was such a little shit. "That wasn't jealousy. It was a warning. Hudson might have you killed."

"Nah. Jinx sees me as a little brother. Hudson is pretty larger than life. I doubt Jinx sees anyone in a sexual light beyond him, except for you, of course. I bet you three made a lot of people fantasize."

"I'm uncomfortable."

Cooper's laughter doubled. He swiped at his eyes. "I'm not a kid."

"Yes. You are." Rocky couldn't emphasize that enough. He was thirty-six. Cooper was young enough to be his son. They weren't about to talk about Rocky's sex life.

"It's not like I'm hitting on you. I was just pointing out the obvious. The three of you together probably turned a lot of heads and sparked a lot of... you know."

Rocky covered his eyes. He couldn't believe this was happening.

. . .

"They're getting married."

Pain sliced through Rocky's chest at Cooper's words. He looked down, expecting to see a knife sticking from his chest. Rocky had to take a breath. He dropped his hand, doing his best to look unaffected. "I know."

Cooper held his stare. "I meant they're getting married really soon. They decided not to have a wedding. So they're eloping—like maybe tomorrow."

It took everything Rocky had to keep breathing. "That's all I ever wanted for them." It was true. He wanted them married and happy, but he had expected to be some part of that. They were moving on without him. It was to be expected, since he wasn't answering their texts. Still, it hurt more than he liked.

"I like you."

. . .

Rocky blinked at Cooper's sudden confession. He didn't know how to take it. "Okay."

"As a friend," Cooper said, expounding on his claim. "You're nice and you took me in, but you're also kind of dumb. Jinx and Hudson obviously still love you. They asked about you and looked wrecked when I told them you're sad."

"You told them I'm sad." Cooper really was an asshole.

"Yes. I told them you're sad because you are, and you're also stupid as fuck. You have two men who want you and you're sitting here with me."

Rocky kind of wanted to punch the kid, but he didn't. "Yeah, well, I like you too as a friend. You shouldn't be alone."

. . .

Cooper moved a piece, checking Rocky's king. "Checkmate. Maybe I should move in with Jinx after all. Then you'll have to come too to keep me from being alone."

"It's not that simple."

Cooper stood. "Actually, I think it's not that hard." Cooper walked away, leaving Rocky alone with his thoughts. Rocky didn't like it. In fact, he hated the silence he used to love. He wondered what Hudson and Jinx were doing tonight. Never in his life had he hurt this badly. He hadn't thought he could lose Jinx and Hudson. Obviously, he had been wrong. Rocky shoved the board from the table, sending chess pieces flying. Cooper was right. Rocky was dumb as hell, but it was too late to change his mind. Hudson and Jinx were moving on without him. They would be married soon. There was no going back. He had lost everything.

TEN

WITH HIS HEART in his throat, Jinx held Hudson's stare while Hudson repeated his vows. On a private beach in Hawaii, in the most beautiful spot Jinx had ever stood, Jinx listened to every word, spoke when prompted to speak, and kissed when told to do so. When their lips met, air finally filled Jinx's lungs. Happy tears fought to escape. It was done. They had done it. He was Jinx Vincent. It was the most wonderful moment of his life.

Hudson pressed his forehead against Jinx's. For a moment, they stared into each other's eyes. They felt more connected than ever before. Jinx soaked up the love.

. . .

"I love you."

Jinx smiled. He swore sometimes Hudson could read his mind. "I love you too."

Bubbles hit Jinx in the face, making him laugh. As their only witness, Tito had taken it upon himself to man every open position in the wedding party. He had thrown flower petals and played ring bearer as well as best man. Now he blew bubbles in their faces while cheering loudly. Hudson snatched Jinx from his feet and ran for the beach house. Tito chased them, still trying to be their one-man party. Jinx imagined they looked insane to the man who had been hired to officiate. Likely he was also relieved to be set free so he could sell the story to the tabloids. All Jinx cared about was the endgame. They were married now. He couldn't believe it. When he had met Hudson, Jinx never thought they would come this far.

. . .

Tito abandoned them at the door of their honeymoon house before he got a show. Their lips met as Hudson crossed the threshold with Jinx in his arms. Jinx's chest filled with pride.

"I'm disappointed in your decision to get married here."

Jinx's head whipped around at the familiar sound of Rocky's voice. Anger, hurt, and something else he didn't want to look too closely at exploded through him at the sight of Rocky.

Hudson let Jinx slip to his feet. He kept his arms wrapped around him, drawing him back against his chest. "Did you picture something different?" Hudson sounded calm. Jinx couldn't decide how to feel. Rocky looked gorgeous. Relaxed. His t-shirt protested his muscles. His shorts showed off his thick legs. Jinx couldn't stop staring at him.

. . .

Rocky's gaze moved between them. "Yeah, I guess I did. I thought you would have a big wedding where Zayn's mom could fuss over you and Cooper could be there. You deserved the limelight and all the guys on the security team wanted to take part."

Hudson lazily stroked Jinx's stomach as he responded. "My dream was always different. I always thought Jinx and I would marry just like this and then we'd have a big commitment ceremony where you joined us for a handfasting-type thing, since you didn't want to get legally married. Of course, that was before you ignored our every attempt to make things right."

Jinx wanted to speak up and have his say too, but he hurt too badly with Rocky standing there.

Rocky pulled a pained face. When he spoke, his voice sounded strained. "I couldn't miss this day. I had to be here."

. . .

"You're supposed to be here." The words burst from Jinx with a passion he couldn't control. They needed to be said. Even if it was Hudson and Jinx's wedding, Rocky had been meant to stand with them. They were supposed to be a team, facing the world and life together.

Hudson kissed Jinx's temple before turning his attention to Rocky. "Jinx is right. You were always supposed to be with us. I'm sorry I drove you away. I'm sorry I'm too much."

Jinx squeezed the arm Hudson had wrapped around his chest. Tears pricked his eyes at the pain in Hudson's voice. He knew Hudson had to say what was in his heart. Hudson's thoughts still stabbed Jinx through the heart. He hated hearing Hudson apologizing for something he couldn't change.

Rocky moved closer. He held Hudson's stare. "You're not too much. I'm not enough. No one taught me to be soft or loving. I'm learning as I go. You're not the issue. I got scared. Not because of you, but because of me. I'm beyond terrified I'll fail you both." Rocky blinked, as if coming back to himself. "I guess I already did that."

"Only if you walk out that door and leave us again," Hudson said, sounding harder than Jinx had ever heard him sound. "If you give up on the love we built, then yeah. You've failed us."

Jinx had his own thoughts to add. "If you want to stay, I expect you to mean it. My heart can't take you giving up every time things get hard. I love you. Losing you is too hard."

Rocky held Jinx's stare with an intensity Jinx had missed more than he dared to admit. No one looked at him the way Rocky did. While beneath Rocky's possessive gaze, Jinx knew he would always have a home. When Rocky spoke, the feeling of being owned doubled. "Make no mistake, I want you two married. I need to know you two will always have each other. But you don't get to do that without me, because you're both mine. You don't get to have this honeymoon and live your lives without me like I don't exist."

Fuck. Jinx couldn't look away. His skin burned with desire. That wasn't enough, though. There had to be a promise of more. "And?" He didn't know what he was digging for, but Rocky hadn't said what Jinx needed to hear to feel secure with Rocky yet.

"I'm not going anywhere." Rocky's gaze moved between them, as if ensuring they understood the gravity of his vow. "I love you both too much to let you go. This is my marriage too, even if I can't sign the papers."

Jinx's eyes fell closed. Air filled his lungs as a weight he hadn't realized he carried lifted from his chest. Rocky had come home.

The air felt like soup, coating his lungs and drowning him. Rocky had never been more scared. All it would take was one of them to say no, and he would be on a plane back to L.A. alone. His life would be over. Nothing mattered to him the way Hudson and Jinx did. He had expected Hudson to be the unforgiving one. It turned out Jinx was the one who openly hurt while staring at Rocky, visibly waiting for Rocky to fix what he had broken by ignoring their pleas and apologies.

Hudson ended up having the words to save them. "Did you only come to watch, or do you plan to participate?"

Rocky's feet moved before his mind caught up. "I love to watch, but I need more." The space between them disappeared as Rocky lunged forward. First, he kissed Hudson and then Jinx before hauling them into his arms. He held on tight while he silently swore he would never let them break again. Then his need to be whole doubled. Rocky tossed Jinx over one shoulder and snagged Hudson's hand. Tito had shown Rocky around earlier on the down low, so Rocky knew which room they would be sharing. He headed that way without looking back. Everything else could wait until after he had his fill of cuddling his babies.

He couldn't stop touching them. His hands stroked every place he could reach as he eased Jinx down onto the bed and climbed in next to him. Then his mouth found Hudson's as he towed Hudson in to join them. He hadn't forgotten the madness they wove when they touched him, but he could never recreate the intensity in his mind. In between Jinx and Hudson, Rocky couldn't do anything other than hang on for the ride. Tongues filled his mouth. Clothes disappeared. His eyes feasted upon the vision Hudson and Jinx created as they kissed. He stared down the line of his body, awed when their kiss included his cock. The sight mesmerized him. Their tongues stroked when they met at his crown. Rocky grabbed the headboard and held on. He had honestly intended to only hold them for a little while. His plans no longer mattered. He was at Jinx and Hudson's mercy. Everything blurred together when Hudson found the lube. The lower half of his body belonged to them.

. . .

Then Jinx's tongue was in Rocky's mouth. Rocky's heart twisted in his chest as love overwhelmed him. He recognized he had gotten lost since he walked away from them—this was real. The three of them weren't playing some complicated game. They were genuinely and completely in love with one another. It wasn't messy. Jinx and Hudson hadn't made it hard for him to come back, because this was where he belonged. There was never any hint of jealousy inside this beautiful triad they had created. No one misunderstood their place. They each belonged to the other equally. Right now, Rocky needed to own their bodies and their souls.

Rocky snagged Jinx's jaw and held his gaze. Jinx's eyes were filled with lust. That was good. Rocky wanted that. "Turn around. I want to watch you kiss Hudson again."

Jinx dutifully turned around, straddling Rocky's body, facing away from him. The moment Rocky had Jinx where he wanted him, he hauled Jinx upward and dove in face first. He tongued Jinx's asshole like it was his last meal. Rocky thrived on the sounds Jinx made as Rocky ate his ass. Then Hudson was on Rocky's cock. His tight asshole sucked Rocky's dick in deep. Rocky lost control. Jinx and Hudson kissed and touched while riding his dick and face. They used him in all the best ways—like he was their personal toy to fuck. He was and always would be. Rocky swapped between attempting to drive Jinx wild and trying to watch Hudson and Jinx stroke each other's cocks. As pressure climbed his shaft, Rocky recognized he would never have enough time to do everything he wanted. He slapped Jinx's ass.

"I want your dick. Give it to me. Fuck my mouth."

Jinx quickly switched positions and straddled Rocky's head. He stared down at Rocky as he led his cock to Rocky's lips. Rocky opened, needing his prize. He sucked and licked while Jinx's hips rolled. Jinx took his pleasure from Rocky's willing mouth. Thinking went out the window. Rocky became nothing more than a giant ball of need. He kneaded Jinx's ass, immersing himself in sucking Jinx's cock while Hudson used Rocky's dick like his personal dildo. Rocky loved every second. The sounds. The smells. He was in carnal heaven. Cum filled his mouth. He swallowed and kept sucking, pulling cries from Jinx that rang from the walls. Rocky dug his heels into the mattress and strained toward release. Hudson's ass felt perfect on his cock. Moans tore from Hudson. Hudson snagged Jinx's hair and forced Jinx's mouth to his. An orgasm struck Rocky like lightning. His body bowed as his dick sawed in and out of Hudson's ass. He fought for air as they collapsed into a sweaty heap of cum, saliva, and sweat. Rocky wanted to bathe in it. He was nowhere near finished with his men. All he needed was to catch his breath.

Air whistled from Hudson's lungs as he struggled to get enough oxygen to survive. The three of them together made magic, but it was a workout. He focused on that because he had never been more frightened of hope. Rocky was here. He talked like he planned to stay, but there were still a thousand things that could go awry. Hudson didn't want to say anything wrong and ruin their new beginning, so he immersed himself in the passion.

· · ·

Jinx didn't seem to share Hudson's fears. The moment he caught his breath, he demanded more answers. "Does this mean you're coming home with us? Please say yes. My heart can't take any more."

Rocky kissed the tip of Jinx's nose. "If you two can forgive me, trust me again, and still want me around full time, I want to be there." He moved to his knees and crawled over Jinx's body, putting Jinx in the middle where he belonged and where Rocky could hold their stares. "We have some stuff to work out, I get that. I want to share a bed with you every night, but I also need to keep working." He held up his hand, stopping Hudson from reminding him he didn't need to work. "It's not about the money. I actually have quite a bit myself since Zayn has always overpaid me and provided my every need. This is about Zayn and a piece of myself I can't relinquish. He depends on me. I can't turn my back on the team I built for him or the friendship he offered me. However, I can move out, go down to working part time, and hand most of my responsibilities off to someone else. I have one request, though."

"Of course," Jinx said at the same time as

Hudson said, "Anything."

Rocky smiled. "It's two requests, really. First, I'd like to bring Cooper with me. He's young and his life is at an important crossroad right now. If I abandon him, he might decide to run back to the streets. I can't live with that."

Hudson didn't even need to think about it. He had already offered Cooper a place once. "Done. What's the second request?"

Rocky's gaze moved between them. He bit his bottom lip, as if scared to speak his thoughts. When he finally answered, he did it fast—like he was afraid his bravery would flee otherwise. "I want that big ceremony handfasting thing you suggested. I want everyone to know you two belong to me."

Jinx brought Rocky's hand to his lips and kissed it. "I want that too."

· · ·

They both looked his way. Hudson laughed. "I'm the one who suggested it. Of course that's what I want."

A smile exploded across Rocky's face. It quickly bled away as he stared at Hudson. "I'm so sorry for everything. You deserved better from me. I wish you had told me about your condition. That doesn't make it your fault I didn't know how to handle a full-blown episode. I just wish I had known and learned how to help before I ruined us."

"Everyone had their share of blame," Jinx said, speaking Hudson's exact thoughts. "I felt vulnerable because I need the security of marriage. My family is gone. I don't want to be alone in the world. Marriage isn't important to you, but it is to me, and I should have voiced that instead of being too scared to lose you."

Hudson jumped in, incapable of letting Jinx carry the weight of everything. "I should've been every bit as open with you as I've been with Jinx. It's just hard to admit that my head is a terrifying place. Jinx is easier to talk to about that, but I never meant to shut you out. I just..." Hudson shrugged. He didn't know how to say he didn't like being seen as weak.

Rocky looked understanding. His heart was in his eyes. "I can't even imagine. It has to be completely terrifying to not know when your mind will turn against you. But you need to know I'll be here when it happens. Jinx will be here when it happens. Most of all, you need to know I can and will force you to stay well. That means taking your meds, going to every doctor's appointment, and letting us in, even when it's ugly."

"Especially when it's ugly," Jinx said, sounding firm.

A lump rose in Hudson's throat. He didn't know what he had done to be this blessed. "I love you both so fucking much. Please hear that and feel it because I know I'm hard to love back. I know I scare people and make them tired, but please know you own my heart." Hudson fought the sudden urge to cry. He had lost so many people over the years because every word he said was true. Hudson's condition exhausted people. He tried really hard to not be a burden, but loving him was work.

Jinx rolled, facing him, and Rocky scooted closer until Jinx was squashed between them. Rocky held them, bringing strength back to their circle. Jinx kissed him. "You're not hard to love at all. You've just been surrounded by weak people."

Rocky nodded. "Agreed. You can't lose us. I might have needed time to think, but you never lost me or exhausted me. This is forever. Get comfortable. Settle in. We're getting ready to make you tired of us."

A laugh burst from Hudson. "Never. I'm retired now. Just think about it. I'm doing all the old superstar things. Writing a tell-all, titled: *This is Me. Suck My Dick*. Guest starring as a washed-up has-been on crime drama shows. The works." Jinx and Rocky laughed. Hudson couldn't stop. "I'm also accepting every talk show invite I get, so I can continue scandalizing the masses with my openness. The world is getting bombarded with pictures of our love and real talk about living with a mental disorder. I don't have a reputation to protect anymore." Hudson's smile slipped away as he stared at the men that he loved more than life. "My life belongs to you two. There's nothing we can't face together."

Jinx blinked back tears. "I know."

Rocky nodded. "We've got this and each other. I love you."

"I love you too," Jinx and Hudson chanted at the same time. As one, they snuggled closer. Hudson closed his eyes and held on. The future was set, and it could wait. They had all the time in the world to plan the rest of their days. Right now, they needed connection. They had found something unique and beautiful, just like each of them. On the surface, they didn't look like they should fit together, but they did. Everything else would work itself out.

ELEVEN

LIGHT GREEN EYES stared a hole through Tito, as if daring Tito to make a move. Cooper was a mystery to Tito. Questions raced to the tip of Tito's tongue. He wanted to ask why Cooper seemed so well-bred for a street rat. The boy did a good job of hiding an expensive education behind random poor grammar. Tito was observant by nature. That was what made him good at his job. Cooper had secrets.

Tito lost himself in the pool of unnaturally light green irises. Cooper's mouth lifted in one corner in an adorable smirk. "Are you studying me or the board?"

. . .

Tito refused to look away and give credence to Cooper's words. "I'm weighing my opponent. Where did you learn to play chess? Do they teach that on the corner of pickpocket lane?"

Cooper's smile grew. "Of course. Right next to knucklebones and card tricks. Everyone should know every good scam if they hope to survive the streets."

Tito pushed the board away and stared harder at Cooper. "Do you consider chess a scam?"

As if needing to prove he wasn't intimidated, Cooper leaned closer too. "It is when a master plays against a novice."

Without looking, Tito made two moves and won. "Which of us is the master?"

A sexy chuckle rumbled from Cooper. His eyes shone bright with happiness. Tito had to take a breath. He had done the math. Not only did Tito have eleven years on Cooper, but he also had a lifetime of experiences older than his new friend. They lived under the same roof. Cooper was like a little brother to Tito's boss. There was so much wrong with the hunger the tiny blond mischief maker stirred in Tito.

Tito sat back and tried to get his fascination under control. "Are you getting excited about Ibiza?"

Cooper nodded. "I'm a lot more excited about joining the guys on their second honeymoon than I am about standing in front of a huge crowd as a groomsman." Cooper swiped his hands on his jeans. "I'm not good at things like that."

"Everyone will be too busy looking at the grooms to worry about us. Plus, I'll be right there with you, keeping you safe."

. . .

With his guard down, Cooper looked even younger than his eighteen years. Tito wanted to protect him. Cooper stared openly at Tito with no coyness whatsoever. "You'll be keeping Hudson safe, not me."

"I won't be the only bodyguard there. Plus, I'm an amazing multitasker."

Cooper's gaze never wavered from Tito's. His foot brushed Tito's beneath the table. Tito couldn't be certain he hadn't been the one who touched Cooper. Cooper's expression turned innocently heated—like he played with a fire he didn't understand. "Who's assigned to keeping you safe from me?"

Tito had pulled Hudson from a lot of sticky situations over the years. Now it was his turn and Tito didn't know what to do. He also wasn't so sure he wanted to be saved. There were worse ways he could ruin his life than with a beautiful street angel. Tito could think of at least a dozen. The only thing

Tito couldn't think about was saying no. He was in a world of trouble.

"Do you think we should tell them we can see them?"

At Jinx's question, Hudson laughed. With Rocky lying on the couch, Jinx was sprawled across Rocky's chest while Hudson sat beneath Rocky's knees. They were snuggled as close as possible while still being comfortable. Hudson stroked Jinx's ass. "I would say something, but then again, they would know we were here if they looked away from each other."

"They should fuck and get it over with," Rocky said, sounding half asleep.

"We can hear you," Tito barked from across the room.

· · ·

Rocky didn't back down. "Good. You should fuck and get it over with. You two are clogging the air with your lust."

Tito stood and headed for the kitchen without looking back.

Hudson went back to stroking Jinx's ass. "You ran him off."

Rocky blew out a raspberry. "Pussy."

Jinx chuckled. "I see you waited until he left the room to say that."

"Fuck yeah, I did. He's almost ten years younger than me and does nothing except work out. I'm not trying to get my ass kicked tonight. Plus, I'm comfortable."

. . .

Hudson scoffed. "I wouldn't let him kick your ass. It's too sexy for that."

Cooper moved from the table to the floor at Hudson's feet. "Are you three excited for tomorrow?"

"Thrilled," Jinx answered first.

"Yep," Hudson and Rocky said at the same time.

Cooper smiled. "You three are so adorable. Everyone's going to take your pictures. You'll be in every magazine. I'm so proud to be standing with you. You're helping other throuples be more open. That's a good thing."

It was a good thing. Hudson hadn't really thought of that aspect. He just wanted to promise his life to his men. It wasn't about anyone else.

. . .

"You're very good at changing the subject," Rocky said, dragging Hudson's mind back to their earlier topic.

Cooper's smile fell. "Please stop. He doesn't look at me that way. No one does. I'm everyone's little brother, and... just don't, okay?"

Rocky reached out and took Cooper's hand. "I'm just messing with you, buddy. Or more to the point, I'm messing with Tito. We're glad you're living here. I wouldn't want you to be uncomfortable living with us."

Cooper nodded. "I know. It's just that you three have each other and Tito feels like the first real friend I've had in a long time. I don't want him to start avoiding me."

"They can't run me off that easily," Tito said, appearing in the doorway with a drink in each hand.

. . .

Hudson smacked Jinx's ass. He recognized their cue. "Let's head to bed. We have a big day tomorrow. It looks like the kids plan to stay up late."

Jinx climbed from Rocky's body and kissed Cooper's cheek. After everyone said their good nights and left Tito and Cooper alone, Rocky, Jinx, and Hudson headed for the bedroom they now shared. They went through their nightly paces and climbed into bed together, the way they did every night. Hudson thrived on the routine. He was healthier than he had been in years and it was completely due to Rocky and Jinx's love. Despite all his progress, Hudson still didn't sleep well. His excitement made things worse. Tomorrow, the whole world would watch them commit to one another and it felt so real.

"Are you okay?"

It was as if Rocky had some sixth sense. He always knew when Hudson had the most trouble sleeping. Hudson smiled into the dark. "Are you? I keep thinking about how you didn't want to be a husband.

Come tomorrow, you'll be as good as one. Not to mention, my lawyers are tying our lives together every bit as legally as a marriage. A part of me keeps worrying you'll back out."

"He's not backing out," Jinx whispered into the dark, as if there was anyone left to disturb.

Rocky snuggled closer, squashing Jinx in between them. "Damn right. I want this. You two are my whole world. I'm ready for all the legal entanglements you can throw my way. This is forever."

A smile tugged at Hudson's lips. His eyelids grew heavy. It was crazy to him how one reassurance from Rocky could make all his troubles disappear. His eyes slipped closed. "I love you both more than the moon." The words sounded thick with sleep, even to his ears. Hudson was pretty sure Rocky and Jinx returned his words, but the warmth of Jinx against his body had Hudson's mind drifting away. He used to be so torn between being happy and being real.

The only person he trusted for years was Tito. Hudson didn't completely understand what choice he had made that had been so right. All he knew was his house was filled with love now. Peace. Happiness. Maybe he was still a bit of mess, but wasn't everyone? At least he wasn't alone. Rocky and Jinx would never let him be alone. Hudson couldn't wait to grow old with his best friends. He couldn't wait to tell the rest of the world to suck his dick. Hudson had chosen happiness. He had chosen to live.

Keep an eye out for the next Candied Crush, *Beautifully Guarded*.

Please consider leaving a review at the retailer where you purchased this book. Reviews really help with a book's visibility, which allows me to continue writing more stories. Thank you, Charity.

ABOUT THE AUTHOR

Charity Parkerson is an award-winning and multi-published author with several companies. Born with no filter from her brain to her mouth, she decided to take this odd quirk and insert it in her characters.

*Eight-time Readers' Favorite Award Winner
   *2015 Passionate Plume Award Finalist
   *2013 Reviewers' Choice Award Winner
   *2012 ARRA Finalist for Favorite Paranormal Romance
   *Five-time winner of The Mistress of the Darkpath

Connect with her online:

—Sign up for my newsletter: https://sendfox.com/charityparkerson
   —Join my readers' group on Facebook: http://bit.ly/CharitysTribe
   —Website: charityparkerson.com

—Facebook: facebook.com/authorCharityParkerson

facebook.com/TheMenofSin

—Twitter: twitter.com/CharityParkerso

—Instagram: Instagram.com/sinnerauthor

—Bookbub: https://www.bookbub.com/authors/charity-parkerson

—Amazon page: author.to/CharityParkerson

—TikTok: http://www.tiktok.com/@charityparkerson

www.ingramcontent.com/pod-product-compliance
Lightning Source LLC
Chambersburg PA
CBHW060151180626
46813CB00007B/2707